Barents Sea

Jerndor!

Tromsø

Niflheim

Thief of Peace's Passage

Jotunheim

Lost Well

The Neighboring Kingdom of Sweden

Norwegian Sea

Malundor

Ellehen

Glade of the Golden Rings

Alheim

Trondheim

Gjallarbrú

Kristiansund

Trolgar

Lago Mountains

Bergen

Oslo

Fredrikstad

Stavanger

Skagerrak Strait

The Enchanted Lands of

Norway

North Sea

The Kingdom of Denmark

A Zaria Fierce Novel

Christoffer Johansen and the Gyllenhammar Flame

Written and Illustrated by
Keira Gillett

E-book ISBN: 978-1-942750-15-4

Paperback ISBN: 978-1-942750-16-1

LCCN: 2022911548

Printed in the United States of America

Reading Order:

Zaria Fierce and the Secret of Gloomwood Forest

Zaria Fierce and the Enchanted Drakeland Sword

Zaria Fierce and the Dragon Keeper's Golden Shoes

Aleks Mickelsen and the Twice-Lost Fairy Well

Aleks Mickelsen and the Call of the White Raven

Aleks Mickelsen and the Eighth Fox Throne War

Christoffer Johansen and the Return to Jötunheim

Christoffer Johansen and the Gyllenhammar Flame

Praise for Zaria Fierce and the Secret of Gloomwood Forest

"Are you in the mood for an old fashioned magical jaunt? Zaria Fierce and the Secret of Gloomwood Forest by Keira Gillett is a classic "perilous adventure" book for middle grade readers." *Jennifer Bardsley, The YA Gal*

"A captivating blending of fantasy storytelling with today's technology. At the base of this tale is deep, abiding friendship that stands the tests of time, adventure and even danger." *Kathy Haw, Goodreads Review*

"If you're looking for an action-packed adventure dipped in fantasy, look no further. This book kept me on my toes with its many cliffhangers and plot twists; it was quite hard to put down at times." *Meredith, All 'Bout Them Books and Stuff*

"This was a really good book with a great setting and cool plot line. I really liked how it didn't hide that Zaria was adopted and she knew it. I also liked how her adoptive parents were nice. You don't see that often in books (as an adopted kid, I like it when adoption is portrayed well)." *Erik, This Kid Reviews Books*

"A great book with vivid descriptions and relatable characters. The main character becomes a strong female lead, and the writing and illustrations make this fantasy world even more real and interesting." *Analee, Book Snacks*

Praise for Zaria Fierce and the Enchanted Drakeland Sword

"The Zaria Fierce series just keeps getting better, with this sequel! This is an awesome fantasy filled with suspense, from the first page to the last! The vivid descriptions combined with the beautiful illustrations make the setting come to life." *Brandi Nyborg, Goodreads Review*

"This is one of the most amazing second books in a trilogy that I've read. I like how empowering the book is, especially on facing your own demons. Just like Zaria." *Danissa, The Booklandia*

"I like how the action begins quickly and Gillett brings the reader up to speed on the plot, no time is wasted in getting these friends off on another adventure through the Norwegian countryside. Oh, and that setting, it's one of the most enjoyable things in reading Gillett's stories. All the lovely rich details of each of the magical kingdoms, each place is unique and highlights the depth of her imagination." *Brenda, Log Cabin Library*

"Zaria is both vulnerable and strong, and very much a role model for my own daughters." *APinFL, Audible Review*

Praise for Zaria Fierce and the Dragon Keeper's Golden Shoes

"The Zaria Fierce trilogy is a fun middle grade adventure with a great message, and *Zaria Fierce and the Dragon Keeper's Golden Shoes* rounds it out perfectly! Zaria and her friends are realistic characters and I thoroughly appreciated the exploration of their friendship and growth as individuals and as a group. I think the Zaria Fierce series deserves a lot more love!" *Nicole, Read Eat Sleep Repeat*

"*Zaria Fierce and the Dragon Keeper's Golden Shoes* was the magical conclusion this trilogy asked for. Filled with action and adventure, Zaria and her friends showed us the importance of teamwork, friendship, and having courage in ourselves. The perfect ending to a fun series, I recommend this to all fantasy lovers, middle school and beyond!" *Emily, Midwestern Book Nerd*

"*Zaria Fierce and the Dragon Keeper's Golden Shoes* was a spectacular conclusion to a great trilogy (though the ending left the door open for more adventures). Filled with magic, a great story line, amazing and real characters, wonderful settings and beautifully explored themes, Keira Gillett created a trilogy that I will always cherish and will visit anytime. If you like The Chronicles of Narnia, *The Hobbit,* The Spiderwick Chronicles or simply love a book filled with Norwegian folklore and fantasy, then this is the ultimate series for you to read, devour and lose yourselves in." *Ner, A Cup of Coffee and a Book*

Praise for Aleks Mickelsen and the Twice-Lost Fairy Well

"You don't realise how much you miss things till they are gone, and this is the case with this series. The characters had a way of worming themselves into my heart and I missed them! Well, they are back and better than ever!!" *Natalie, Book Lover's Life*

"I loved the first three Zaria books and I have to say I'm even more in love with Aleks! I was surprised by the many twists and turns of the book and loved catching up with all the new and old characters. This book would be a great gift for any young teenager and it's a great read for an adult like myself." *Rusty Forsmark, Amazon Review*

"There is so much that I loved about this story. Aleks is one of my favorite characters and I am so excited that he is getting his own stories so that readers can learn more about him and go on this journey of self-discovery along with him and his friends." *Bridgett, Little Bee's Reads*

"I must find a way to sneak a stargazer along with a thousand pesky request letters in the mail to the author to try to get the next book to come out faster!" *Ronald Shaw, Audible Review*

Praise for Aleks Mickelsen and the Call of the White Raven

"This volume of the Zaria Fierce series feels like a fun camping trip. A combination of an adventure and a love story. Entertaining from beginning to end and recommended." *Christian, Audible Review*

"Everything you love about the Zaria Fierce books is here: the strong friendships, the nonstop adventure, the magical creatures, and the hero's quest are all here, waiting for fantasy lovers to join them. Keira Gillett's at the height of her storytelling here;" *Rosemary, Mom Read It*

"I really enjoyed this next book. Aleks is definitely becoming my favorite character in the series. Seeing him face his fear, and his fate, in accepting who he is, has made me think, and reminds me of my own individual quest for identity." *Daniel, Audible Review*

Praise for Aleks Mickelsen and the Eighth Fox Throne War

"From the opening sentence of the prologue to the final paragraph, you know you are in a fierce adventure. Having been with the series since the beginning, it has been wonderful following our group through all the action! *Aleks Mickelsen and the Eighth Fox Throne War* abounds with magic and if fey politics don't get you killed, the dragon just might … or a beautiful fairy's father… Settle in and get ready for a great story from one of my favorite authors." *Tammy Spencer, Goodreads Review*

"I held my breath many times reading this book. The challenges are nonstop. You'll find plenty of fierce battles and extremely scary creatures. But, as always in this series, friendship, cooperation, and just the right amount of humor offer hope in the darkest of times." *Patricia Mather Parker, Author of The Abode*

"Keira does it again in the third Aleks Mickelsen book! Full of adventure, the story continues on as the gang tries to fool the plans of Fritjof, a dragon that is sneakier than a snake. Keira's writing always impresses me… A highly enjoyable read for all ages!" *Amanda, Goodreads Review*

Praise for Christoffer Johansen and the Return to Jötunheim

"There's lots of questing, and at the heart of the novels are the relationships between all of the characters. I really like how the stories are broken down into each character's story arc. Christoffer doesn't see himself as the hero of the story, not having any magical powers, but his words are probably his best weapon. He's the peacekeeper between his friends, in tune with everyone's emotions, and first to make a joke or help to defuse tension. I quite enjoy watching his story evolve." *Brenda, Log Cabin Library*

"I feel this series gets better and better with every new audiobook. The story is very good (sometimes it feels like a fairy tale to me), and Michele Carpenter has again done a great job narrating it." *Christian, Audible Review*

"We just can't get enough of this series. We totally love the character." *Book Lover, Audible Review*

Dedication:

2021 In loving memory of my brother. Kind, loyal, generous, and a jokester. Christoffer would be proud to call you his wingman, even if your humor is different than his. Thank you for always supporting me. You'll always be in my heart and part of my world.

2022 In loving memory of my mother. Steadfast, kind, giving, my dearest friend, and my staunchest supporter, a little bit of you will always be in these pages. Thank you for going on every adventure and always cheering me on to greater heights. I love you to the moon and back.

Special Thanks:

I couldn't have published this book without my beta readers, sensitivity readers, volunteers, and editor-in-chief. You make the world a brighter place. Thank you to Tammy, Aspen, Kai, Jen, Michele, and Karen. You are some of the most extraordinary people I know, and I am grateful for your help with this book.

To Readers:

You are stronger, braver, and kinder than you think. May your sorrows be few and your joys be abundant. May all your fears melt like dew in sunshine, so that even the memory of them disappears. May your cup be always full of love, laughter, and delight.

Table of Contents

Prologue: Riding the High..19

Chapter One: Collecting Olaf.......................................27

Chapter Two: Kraken Good Time 47

Chapter Three: The Svefnthorn 67

Chapter Four: It's Troll, Not Toll, Bridge 87

Chapter Five: The Two-Headed Troll......................105

Chapter Six: The Gulley...123

Chapter Seven: Odd Couple 141

Chapter Eight: A New Mission 163

Chapter Nine: Grizzle's Tale......................................185

Chapter Ten: The Witch's Prize 205

Chapter Eleven: The Fear Upon the Hill.................225

Chapter Twelve: Ghouls Make for Terrible Pets....243

Chapter Thirteen: My Good Friend "Hank"...........263

Chapter Fourteen: The Gyllenhammar Flame 281

Epilogue: Dwarvish Metallurgy Unlocked..............299

Prologue: Riding the High

Even though it was well past midnight Christoffer was not tired at all. Down in the galley he was still riding the high of victory – retelling his escapade of running the oars on a Viking longboat, laughing raucously at jokes (both his and others), and flirting outrageously with a feisty ellefolken girl.

"I wish I could've had a go," she said, rife with envy, her chin propped carelessly on one tiny fist. She twirled a coin between her fingers and flipped it. "Heads or tails?"

"Uh tails," Christoffer guessed.

"Ooo, heads, wrong again," she teased. "At least you're cute."

"You're cute," he told her, with a bit of saccharine sweetness, essentially driving away anyone else who'd been hanging around. The galley crew went back to cleaning up from the night's meal and prepping for tomorrow's.

Phoebe was the sort of girl who dove into adventure headfirst. One of her short antlers was wrapped in bandages, healing from some recent scrimshaw, which is like a tattoo on bone. She refused to declare what the finished piece would be and told everyone it was everything from the face of her true love to a ghoul's regurgitated meal. She blithely pointed out a thin white scar that ran through her right eyebrow, bisecting it at the side. "I got it while wrestling an ogre who wanted to use the main mast as a scratching post. I told him to stop, and he didn't like it. Knocked me in the temple with his club." That, too, seemed farfetched, but it made for a hell of a conversation starter.

They were aboard the *Ursula*, and its captain, Bjarke, would take anyone on as passengers so long as they had funds. Ogres were nasty oversized humanoids with enough stink in one foot alone to make it seem Bjarke was ferrying a garbage barge. Considering the vessel was the river-troll's pride and joy, the only way for

Phoebe's story to make sense was if money was involved. "At least tell me Bjarke overcharged the oaf," he said.

"Aye, he did, and made him pay for damages, too," she giggled. "But I kind of like it, you know? Gives me face character."

"Warns the next ogre to think twice," he agreed, leaning on the counter.

She pulled out an old-fashioned pocket watch and clicked it open, frowning unhappily. "Me watch is coming up. I'll need to leave soon."

"Stay a little longer?" he wheedled, picking up a jug of coffee. "Have another cup, so you can stay awake."

"These are me normal hours. The thing with the raven was like waking up at the crack of dawn."

"Can the dawn crack?" he asked, pouring them both a cup anyway. "Does it have a butt?"

"But of course," she replied, winking. "You can even kiss up to it."

He inhaled the fragrant liquid and took a sip. "I'll bite. Where's the dawn's butt?"

"Oh, she doesn't like biting."

"She's missing out," he said, giving her a saucy wink.

She laughed in his face. "Tell you what, if you look closely, you'll find her butt where the sky kisses the sea."

"The horizon," he answered. "Too easy."

"If you're being literal," she teased. "However, you asked if there was a crack and I obligingly told you how to locate it. Thanks for the cup, cutie."

Christoffer sighed forlornly as Phoebe left, taking with her a bit of that sunshine they'd been discussing. It had been nice flirting with a girl his own age again. Of course, ellefolken nearly always looked young. Age was hard to pinpoint with them (and also elves) for they lived long lives. She might look like she was eighteen, but she could easily have been as many years as his mother. He didn't really fancy himself the life of Oedipus.

Finishing his own cup of coffee in one large swallow, he then placed their dishes in the sink along with the nearly empty pot. Waving goodnight to the galley at large Christoffer slipped out and winded his way through the narrow hall, up a flight of stairs, making his way toward his bunk with Filip and Henrik.

He found the room softly lit by a dimmed lamp and Henrik sitting upright in bed writing in a journal. Filip, he noted was sound asleep, and quiet, his perpetual snores silenced by a proper sleeping configuration with a dam of pillows propping his head so it wasn't flat.

"Hey," he greeted, careful to keep his voice pitched low to not waken their friend. "You're up late."

Henrik nodded. "I'm recording the events of the last few days so when I consult the Golden Kings later, I won't have forgotten anything."

"Where's Defender?" he asked, looking around for his loyal canine companion.

"With Zaria," Henrik replied.

"That traitor," he laughed, stripping off his crusty, briny clothes.

Christoffer took a quick shower before settling into bed. Like Henrik, his thoughts also swirled, but he preferred sorting them out in his head versus on paper. The past few days had been a whirlwind of activity from running into the river-troll Olaf with his concerns about the Glomma drying out, and presumptuous goblins encroaching on his territory, to getting tasked by Queen Helena of the Under Realm to replace the broken Drakeland Sword to acrimonious meetings with the giant tribe of Seiland Island and finally beating a talkative white raven named Skorri in a game of wits, perspicacity, and brawn.

Winning the raven's challenges was the first true step in the goal to replace the sword. Having secured Skorri's cooperation in meeting Master Brown, the brownie caretaker living under the elf kingdom of Álfheim, they could clear a debt Henrik owed. How that would precisely help them, only the witch of the woods knew, but Henrik trusted her judgement and advice. To wit they were heading to Master Brown, but, first, a side trip.

Tomorrow, they were rendezvousing with Olaf. Hopefully, he'd been able to persuade Oskar the Elevated of the importance of joining forces. Signs were springing up everywhere that another dragon needed to be stopped from escaping the Under Realm and destroying the earth as they knew it. Christoffer didn't envy the burden placed on Henrik's shoulders to do just that... although perhaps Henrik didn't know it was his burden. Perhaps he thought it would again fall to Zaria.

As sleep began to overtake him, Christoffer's thoughts tumbled between Phoebe, Pia – another ellefolken girl he'd met a few days before, and the nameless hulder who nearly kissed him. He frowned and forcibly woke up enough to turn over to his side, punching the pillow to conform better to his neck. Comfortable, sleep began to weigh down his eyelids again and a yawn escaped. He tried not to think, not wanting to dream; but, as unconsciousness claimed him, a haunting, lilting voice, singing tauntingly, "*Know ye are mine forever, and grant an eternal kiss to me,*" tried to overtake his fading thoughts. Forget kissing the dawn, when a hulder wanted to trade saliva – or blood – it was nearly unthinkable to say no.

Chapter One: Collecting Olaf

A pair of succulent ruby red lips disturbed his dreams, leaving Christoffer restless and feeling ill-used. Both vivid and troubling, he was reminded again of how much he had wanted to believe in the illusion of goodness and desire she projected. She was a clever huntress, and he a far too willing victim. Even in his dreams he wanted to meet her halfway, more than halfway if he was honest.

Drenched in sweat and dismayed, he woke to stare blankly at the ceiling. "Not real," he whispered.

Even though, the feelings of want and need were all too real. He closed his eyes and kicked the sheets away, finding them too cloying and hot.

The sound of bells tolling penetrated his brooding thoughts. Were they near land? Wasn't it too early for a church to ring its bells? Before he could figure it out the ship heaved upward as if something massive pushed it skyward from below.

Warning bells! he frantically figured out as he floated above his bed and crashed heavily to the ground.

Shouts of pain and confusion rang out from Henrik and Filip as the ship dropped suddenly. It felt like the floor fell from beneath them, a tricky thing to do when they were already braced against it on hands and knees.

"Ahh!" they screamed as the *Ursula* creaked and groaned around them ominously, threatening to split in half.

Lamplight flickered on. Henrik braced against the end table, his hand on the knob adjusting the wick's brightness. A quick glance around the room showed all the furniture nailed into place still secure – only he and his friends, their bedding and backpacks were flung hither and yon.

"What was that?" Filip asked, the whites of his eyes visible from across the room.

"A reef, maybe?" Christoffer asked, reaching for his bag with his foot, unwilling to let go of the bed leg.

"An iceberg," Filip offered, standing on shaking legs. He went to the door and flung it open, startling when he saw Zaria and the others readying to knock.

"Woof!" Defender barked upon seeing Christoffer, surging against Aleks' grip. The fey king let him go.

"Hey buddy," he said laughingly when greeted by excited barks and energetic licks.

"What say you?" Filip asked, inviting them into the room.

"Another ship?" suggested Aleks.

"Or the kraken," Christoffer teased, his worry and fear greatly diminished upon seeing his friends safe and secure and having his dog with him.

"Don't joke," Geirr admonished, holding the wall to stay upright.

"I don't know what to think," Zaria said, having heard all the group's conjectures.

Henrik, dragged on his golden antlered cloak and secured the fastening. "I think we need to consult with Bjarke."

The ship lurched drunkenly again, causing them to stumble in all directions. Defender whined, Geirr moaned, and Christoffer immediately sought to balance both. He propped up his friend on one side. Aleks supported the other and they half-carried-half-dragged him toward the hatch with his dog sticking close to his legs, pressed tight against his side.

"I think I'm going to be sick," Geirr moaned, his head wobbling on his neck like a demented bobblehead.

Christoffer made a face. "Just aim for anywhere but my shoes, okay? I don't know why but every adventure involves something with shoes. Golden shoes for Zaria, yucky mucky shoes for Aleks, I don't want puke shoes. Got it?"

Half moan, half laugh, the taller teen said, "No promises."

"Hold on," Aleks said, soothingly. "Fresh air just ahead."

Emerging from the corridor they discovered the crew in a state of controlled urgency. Everyone hustled about, calling to each other. Ellefolken and elves were manning posts, but not ones Christoffer had seen them man before. These were emergency positions and all hands were on deck.

One rang the bell in a very specific interval, calling out the warning. Crew scurried up the masts and aimed spotlights on the water. Others took positions beside canons, which until now, he'd always assumed were decoration. Who after all would dare to pirate a troll's sailing vessel? Someone – or something – crazier or stronger than the captain.

Bjarke stood at the helm shouting orders, which all who heard scrambled to obey. Fear in varying degrees lay like a shroud over the scene. Faces were drawn tight as everyone worked diligently at their appointed tasks. Eyes strayed to the churning water, straining to see their hidden foe.

From across the way, Christoffer saw Phoebe running, carrying – of all things – harpoons, using the leather apron she wore to hold them. Her straight blonde hair was pulled back, revealing shaved sides. Beside her ran another ellefolken girl with slashing brows and a fierce expression. They were armed to kill.

"Phoebe, oy, over here!" he yelled, waving.

She looked their way and nodded to her companion. They parted and Phoebe waited, anxious and tense. Christoffer shrugged out from under Geirr's heavy arm and hurried over, Defender on his heels, and huffing low warnings, on high alert due to the ship's atmosphere.

"What's happening? Is there a fire?" he asked.

She shook her head, showing him the harpoons. "According to the signal, we're under attack."

He asked, "What would attack the *Ursula*?"

"The kraken," she explained, darting a glance to the water below.

"Has anybody seen it?" asked Henrik, joining them.

"Nobody's laid eyes on it yet, but I know it's out there, waiting and biding its time."

"If you haven't seen it, then how do you know it's the kraken?" pressed the Stag Lord, frowning.

"What else could toss around a ship like *Ursula*?" she countered. "This is no ordinary vessel."

"What can be done to help?" Christoffer asked, overriding the ellefolken prince's doubts, when it looked like he would argue the point further.

"We need more fire power."

"Where are me harpoons?" bellowed Bjarke, his visage fiercer and scarier then Christoffer had ever seen. He looked like a villainous pirate; the affable captain gone. The stakes were too high for niceties.

"I have to go," Phoebe said, shifting her load. "The ammo crates spilled over below deck. We're trying to get up as many loads as we can."

"We'll head there and help," he assured her. "Deliver these and we'll be back soon with more."

Henrik nodded, agreeing with the plan and motioned to him to follow. Zaria offered to stay with Geirr above deck, relieving Aleks from supervising their unsteady friend. Dodging the crew, they ran back the way they'd come, going the opposite direction from the main flow of traffic. Aleks cut in front and following him they managed to slide between the gaps, avoiding the harried sailors and their sharp, awkward burdens.

Below deck they headed toward the galley and hold opposite their sleeping quarters. An elvish woman with green and brown face tattoos and a heavy leather coat pierced all over with fish hooks directed those going into the hold.

"Get those in that crate there. Bjarke called for that caliber. Hurry up. Every second counts. We're under attack, folks," she shouted to someone they couldn't see and nodded to a short boy who ran past her with an armload.

"How can we help?" Henrik asked, pausing by the woman, while peering over her into the room beyond.

"Help Gwen with the ammunition," she ordered. "The rest of you lot grab some more harpoons."

Christoffer raced into the room, picking his way across several damaged barrels and crates. Food stuffs, fabrics, furniture, and raw materials were scattered everywhere, bruised and busted. Reaching a tipped-over crate, he began to scoop an armful of ammunition when Filip joined him. The ship heaved and rolled, and he lost several harpoons as they crashed down around them. One sliced through Filip's pant leg. He grabbed it and frowned at the torn scrap of cloth.

"I think it's better if we put all these back into the crate and then take that upstairs."

The ship tilted so far to the side that Christoffer nearly fell on top of the ones he was carrying. Getting stabbed through the chest was not on his agenda for this adventure. Everything crashed down when the ship righted itself heavily.

"Good idea, let's get out of here before we are shish kabobbed on these things," he said, shoving the harpoons haphazardly into the crate before the next wave or tentacle or whatever lurched the ship again.

Somehow, they managed to get most of them back into the crate and hauled it upright, before that happened. With one of them on either side, they began maneuvering their load of ammunition back to the fishhook lady. They could see Aleks juggling an armful while working his way back across the room. Henrik was gone, perhaps back upstairs with the unseen Gwen and the ammo.

"Don't dawdle, don't dawdle," shouted the elf as they drew near. "Get those upstairs now. Now!"

Christoffer hastened his step, jogging backwards. "I'm trusting you to not let me collide with anything."

"It's a straight hallway," Filip said, rolling his eyes.

"Let me know if anyone comes up behind me."

"I'm sure they'll get out of the way," Aleks said, running ahead.

The ship lurched again and cries could be heard, including from their own mouths as they bounced hard off the walls like a pinball against a bumper. Running at an angle down the hall, they reached the stairs and hustled up them. At the top, an echoing boom rattled the air, startling them both. Juggling their load, they oriented themselves as splashes and more explosions resounded from cannons and harpoons being fired.

Following the cries for more harpoons, they dropped their crate by a pair of elves who immediately took over, grabbing one and loading it into the front muzzle. Spotlights danced around, casting the ship's deck in a weird almost club-like atmosphere.

"There, Captain!" shouted one of the sailors pointing from the crow's nest.

Christoffer watched as the men beside them fired the harpoon gun into the water after a dark shape. Incongruous with where his eyes showed him was the threat, the ship roiled and rolled in the opposite direction sending him end over end backwards and into the railing on the other side.

He felt pressure on his collar, choking him, as a force held him in limbo halfway over the water. Looking back, he saw Geirr clutching his shirt collar with grim determination etched across his pallid brow. In light of saving him, seasickness was forgotten, that is until he tried to speak. The ship fell back into place and Geirr moaned, head hanging over the side of the railing and it was Christoffer's turn to hold him steady.

"Hold your fire!" cried Zaria, suddenly.

"Too late," Christoffer murmured as Geirr vomited over the rail.

Their sorceress friend sent out half a dozen flares into the sky, washing the scene in purple. "It's not the kraken," she yelled, waving her hands frantically for everyone to stop.

"What is going on now?" Bjarke demanded, stomping over to the rail to peer below. "If it's not the kraken, what is it?"

"Whales," she said grimly. "We're being attacked by humpback whales."

Sure enough, when Christoffer looked over the rails now, he caught sight of a tail flipping as a whale dived below, a bright blue symbol emblazoned on its fluke. This was not an ordinary pod of humpback whales.

"Oskar the Elevated goes too far," Bjarke growled. "These waters are mine. Mine. Not his."

"Someone should try telling him that," Christoffer said, pointing ahead.

In the distance, Seiland's giants towered menacingly from the cliffs, silhouetted against the pinking sky. Dawn's rays glanced across their feet, leaving their faces cloaked in shadows. Trapped between them, captive and bound, lay Olaf. Christoffer couldn't be certain from this distance, but it looked like he'd been badly beaten. Surely their friends amongst the giants had protested such treatment. He scanned the cliff face for them, but could not spy them.

This did not bode well for the safety of the magical realm. What does one do when an ally for the good team refuses to honor the call for aid? Worse, what does one do when they attack a friendly delegate and treat him in such poor fashion? They could not afford to war amongst each other. Hadn't everyone seen that when Aleks fought to unite Niffleheim against Fritjof? If the fey, of all races, could do it, why couldn't the giants, who persistently preached prudence?

"This is wrong," Zaria said coldly, her purple gaze flinty and fists clenched tight. "I'm going over there."

"Take me with you," Henrik said at once, flexing his hand on his sword hilt. "Oskar's affronted more than just the Under Realm with his actions."

"Aye," agreed Bjarke, his clawed hands gripping the railing so tightly his scaly knuckles bleached of color and the wood creaked in protest. "It's time he remembers who controls these waters. We all be going, Princess."

He closed his glowing neon eyes and inhaled deeply. A low hum swelled as the waters churned in slow, heavy swirls. Rising higher and higher the cyclone lifted the ship straight up, creating a tower of water. Above the whales, the watery column moved swift and sure meeting little resistance as the wind buffeted around them filling the sails.

The sudden difference in height was like being hurdled upwards on the platform Master Brown controlled. Back then, it had been on a safe and secure, thoroughly tested, mechanically controlled, water geyser shooting upward from the outer reaches of Trolgar into the heart of Álfheim. This time, under Bjarke's power, they loomed like a skyscraper against the clouds, nearly kissing them, and teetering precariously on the edge of disaster, ready to collapse.

"I don't like this," Geirr said, closing his eyes, his worries compounded by the soaring height, rocking ship, and whipping wind. Christoffer could see his pulse beat rapidly at his throat as panic swelled in tandem with the cyclone.

"Nice, even breaths," Aleks said, coaching their unsettled friend. "Think of it like flying. It's not much different than a cockpit is it?"

"The airplane is more secure," he muttered.

"How so? You still have to deal with turbulence and there's nothing supporting the plane except wind," Christoffer said, his mind only partially on the conversation as excitement permeated his every extremity at this new facet of river-troll magic revealed.

"I'm in control," Geirr explained, wiping sweat and briny flecks of saltwater from his brow.

"Maybe Bjarke will let you hold the helm?" Christoffer offered.

"Helmsman or no," the river-troll intoned darkly, "make no mistake, me ship obeys me just like these waters. This is my territory and only at my benevolence can you cross it."

"River-trolls and their tolls, am I right?" he asked Zaria, nudging her with his elbow and waggling his eyebrows.

"Christoffer," she warned, eyeing him sidelong. "We have grave matters to attend to; this isn't the time."

"It's always the time for some levity," he informed her. "Olaf will be all right, he has us. We'll retrieve him from their care and set him to rights. You'll see."

"I wish I had your optimism," she said, tense and withdrawn beside him. "I don't know how to persuade

Oskar any more than Olaf did, and you can see for yourself how well that turned out for him."

"What if seeing Oskar like this convinces one of the others to take over the High Court of Jötunheim? Wouldn't that be a good thing?" Aleks asked. "I think Christoffer is right to be optimistic."

"A kingdom we need as an ally fighting against itself doesn't seem like it would be a good thing," she murmured.

"However, toppling an unjust ruler is. The giants pride themselves on having wise rulers. They will see how unwise he is being. You don't turn your back on alliances because of your enemies' actions. That's absurd and ruinous."

Henrik inclined his head thoughtfully. "If the seed isn't already sown, perhaps we can plant the idea ourselves."

The ship crested to a stop as the wave halted in line with the tops of the cliffs. Flecks of water shimmered in the air, forever falling, but never hitting the ground or the cliff face. With the sun blocked by their large bodies, the giants squinted and shielded their craggy faces trying to find them in the shadows. Their angry scowls did not for one moment make Christoffer think they would overthrow their ruler. They seemed to be in sync with his madness.

"Give me back me cousin," Bjarke growled, his portly frame quivering with suppressed rage, so unlike the jovial butterball who greeted them; it was like they were two different people... er... trolden.

Olaf groaned at the demand, trying to speak. He was a mess of welts and bruises with one eye swollen shut and his gnarled hands skewed grotesquely around busted knuckles. The ring which Queen Helena had given the river-troll lay broken on the ground, its cracked stone clutched fiercely in his hand. On meeting Zaria's stricken gaze, Olaf's eyes filled with tears, and he broke into sobs, hiding his grief in the crook of his elbow.

Purple flames erupted around the scene as Zaria leveled a condemning glower across the lot of giants. One or two winced in shame, but it was too late.

"You disgust me," she seethed. The air crackled uncomfortably against Christoffer's skin. It clearly took every ounce of her control not to lash out at the tribe before her. "Where is Oskar? How does he try to defend his actions? How do you?"

One of the younger giants, so assumed due to the lack of crags or pits in his smooth stone face, bristled at the dressing down. His lips parted to speak, ready to cut the princess down to size, but she zapped him before his mouth even fully opened, sealing it shut. His eyes widened in horror and several giants nearby who witnessed the magic took a step back in fright.

The one comforting the magically speechless giant was not the only one with courage left to glare, but definitely was the only one willing to speak. His youthful voice rumbled like a rockslide, tempestuous and full of callous disregard for safety – his own or others. "You dare attack us?"

The words were threatening and seemed to bolster the giants who had been cowed by Zaria's display of magic. She forced herself to unclench her fists. "Queen Helena sent an emissary to relay news that impacts not only the High Court of Jötunheim and all giant tribes which fall under its rule, but every nation magical and mundane. You did not treat him with the respect owed his position, and your lack of respect is a slight against her."

Oskar appeared behind the giants, partially hidden from view by their bulk. He laid a steady, fatherly hand on the callow youth and answered in his stead. "You think to sway us with more lies? This river-troll is unfaithful, untrustworthy, and unreliable. He is the source of all our troubles."

"You are not worthy of your heritage, your name, or your place amongst the nations of Norway." She looked to the other giants and back to Oskar. "Are you so brainwashed by *them*?" she asked, hollow with grief.

"Them?" sneered Oskar. "I know not of whom you speak."

Aleks gazed unflinchingly at the crowd. In his stateliest commanding voice, he beseeched them to see reason. "Have the dragons won you to their side? They're the source of all our troubles, not Olaf. He is free from their influence, trusted and protected by allies. Do not discount what he's contributed for all our safety."

"If it weren't for him, my wife and our queen would still be among us," sneered Oskar, and the giants around nodded in agreement.

"Koll would have found a way to break free regardless," Christoffer said. "Dragons are relentless."

"Koll didn't have to find a way. He had Olaf."

"Olaf was just as much a victim," Zaria protested. "He was not himself."

Her defense of the river-troll seemed at odds with the facts, but of them all she would know. The dragon had nearly warped her as well – preying on her emotions and twisting them to his benefit. Christoffer knew all this, but having been kidnapped by the troll he could understand Oskar's point too, but not the giant's actions. Those were reprehensible.

"They follow without thought," Henrik stated when the silence stretched uncomfortably long and the mutinous glare from Oskar dimmed not one watt. The Stag Lord straightened to his full height, relaxing his ruthless grip from the hilt of his sword. "Too young and too green to have learned much critical thinking. It is not their fault."

"Ignorance is no excuse," Aleks said. "Right and wrong are not that oblique."

"Ye know full well what ye are doing, don't ye, yer Elevated," Bjarke guessed, bristling. "Ye will return me cousin forthwith or face the full wrath of a river-troll. What will yer precious whales do without water to swim in?"

Oskar sneered, "The giants of Jötunheim will not bow down to the capricious whims and fancies of little lords and ladies who think they're without fault."

"Do I need to threaten twice?" Bjarke hissed.

Casually, as if it cost him nothing, though it clearly did, because Christoffer saw his eye twitch, the giant ruler said with a sneer, "Release him."

As soon as the words left his mouth, a giant female roughly hauled Olaf to his feet and shoved him toward the floating *Ursula*. He stumbled to them on injured feet. Gnarled hands clutched the cracked stone tightly, refusing to part with it. Matted hair, caked with blood, stuck to his face.

"Princess," he murmured brokenly the moment his eyes met hers.

"It's all right," she shushed him, gripping his hands and tenderly squeezing them.

His yellow eyes welled with tears as Christoffer and Aleks hauled him aboard. She then summoned the ring's setting from the ground and with a deliberate wave at the giants, spooking them, released the magical binding on the immature giant. At their wide eyes and blank uncomprehending visages, she raised a brow of defiance.

"Unlike others here, I am not a monster."

Chapter Two: Kraken Good Time

"You are one badass princess," Christoffer enthused as the tower of water shrank and the ship was spirited away from the cliffs.

Ursula dipped and swayed as the waters rapidly receded, melting back into the ocean currents like a glacier under the hot sun. When the ship returned to its normal position on the waves, Geirr released his death grip on the rail and actually looked relieved instead of seasick, his color nearly back to normal.

Surveying the disappearing cliffs, a deep frown marring his brow, Geirr asked, "What now?"

"We get Olaf the care he needs," Zaria said, tucking an arm through the river-troll's, keeping him close.

"Olaf be fine, Princess," he said gruffly, looking abashed. "You need not be fussing over me."

"Stuff and nonsense," she proclaimed, securing him to her more readily and leading him back below deck.

"I'll have a bath drawn for ye," Bjarke stated, raking his gaze over his cousin. "Ye be needing to wash up at the very least."

"It'll be restorative," Zaria agreed. "Perhaps a hearty repast in the dining hall? What sounds good?"

Olaf stared down at his clenched fist. "I not be deserving of such things. I be failing at my tasks."

"We don't see it that way," Christoffer said, speaking for them all. "Who knew that we'd lost an ally?"

"Have they really been our ally?" asked Aleks. At Henrik's puzzled look, he continued, "Hear me out. It's just as we have all said. The giants spurned helping when it came to rescuing Henrik. They've refused trades and support unless proof of a dragon is shoved down their overly large throats, and even then, it seems like the support is overwhelmingly begrudged."

"I think Mr. Overwhelming would have something to say to that," Christoffer joked, thinking of the young giant from a neighboring tribe who'd readily assisted them before in various ways.

"That's just it, isn't it?" Aleks pressed. "Why is the High Court of Jötunheim so reticent when the lower courts are supportive? Maybe it is time for them to host their own Firething and reestablish their hierarchy. Oskar is compromised and so is his tribe."

Zaria pursed her lips thoughtfully. Thinking aloud, she said, "They have lost many voices of calming and measured influence."

"It's not something we can push for, though," said the Stag Lord. "That endangers our treaties and strips from them their autonomy."

"Be that as it may, let us table this discussion for later," Bjarke advised, escorting a wilted Olaf through the threshold of the captain's suite. "We shall reconvene later when Olaf is recovered."

"Aye, aye, Captain," Christoffer saluted as the door shut between them.

"He's not a pirate," Geirr said, rolling his eyes.

He shrugged and clapped his hands. "No, he's a river-troll. Did you see what he did earlier? Reversing the whirlpool magic and shooting it up as a column? Zaria you have to try that sometime."

She smiled and shook her head. "I'll leave river-troll magic to river-trolls."

"You can do anything and you choose to do nothing? Aleks, what do you say, man?"

Aleks rolled his eyes. "I would not waste a wish on something so useless."

"Useless?" he choked. "You guys. Think of the possibilities. You could fire water cannons at your enemies or put out wildfires or stop a flood or –"

"Cause one," said Aleks, arching an eyebrow.

"I'm pretty sure water doesn't work that way," Christoffer refuted. "Since it's wet."

"Not the wildfires, you goose, a flood," Zaria said laughing. "Enough magic talk. We should prepare for the next leg of our journey. We disembark tomorrow mid-morning. We need to organize and pack."

"With a wave of your finger that could be accomplished in a jiffy."

"You never quit," she mused wryly.

"And neither should you," he said. "Where would we have been without you learning to teleport or throw fireballs, or shut up annoying giants by sealing their mouths shut? Where did you learn that last one, by the way?"

"I don't know, I just got so mad," she said sheepishly. "That's not who I am; I should've apologized."

"No you shouldn't have," Christoffer said.

"He does have a point Zar-Zar," Filip said. "Don't do things you're uncomfortable doing, but don't avoid trying because you're unsure how it'll turn out."

"Same goes for you, Aleks," said Geirr, meaningfully.

"All right, all right, we'll consider it. Happy?" the fey king grumbled.

"Go team humans," Christoffer cheered, high fiving the other two. "We'll turn these two curmudgeons into wizards yet."

"Wizards?" Zaria said archly, purple magic sparkling at her fingertips.

Christoffer took the cue, grabbing Geirr and Filip by the arms and hustling them down the corridor. Looking back over his shoulder, he grinned and singsonged, "No time to stay and chat; we've got packing to do."

"I'm sure he meant magic users," Filip said consolingly as he was tugged along.

"Magic wielding legends!" Christoffer called over his shoulder.

"They're already legends," Henrik said. "They slayed dragons."

"That was yesterday, this is today," he retorted.

"That guy is a menace," Aleks huffed.

"He may be a menace who's right," Zaria worried, her words following them as they rounded the corner.

Later, when everyone was preparing for bed, Christoffer took the belt from his pants and wrapped it around the ropes of his hammock, creating a makeshift restraint. Henrik eyed it wordlessly and continued to write in his journal, the pen scratching away as if it had a score to settle. Filip had no such compunction and instantly questioned the use of the belt as he tied himself in place.

"I've no desire to crash to the floor again tonight."

Filip snorted. "We're out of giant territory; what are you expecting to happen? The boat to capsize due to rogue whales?"

Henrik closed his journal, stowing it in his bag. "Oskar's influence over creatures of the sea starts and ends with the whales in his pod."

"Funny that you should mention creatures of the sea," Christoffer said, flipping the blanket over his legs. "I've heard we've got plenty of dangerous things to worry about in these currents."

Filip groaned. "Don't go inviting trouble."

"Trouble finds us, remember?" he said defensively. "Look I'm just being prepared that's all. It's your skull if you choose not to get strapped in, I can't force you to do it."

"What about Defender?" questioned Henrik, looking toward the watchful dog curled up on the floor in the corner. "Are you not going to do the same for him?"

Christoffer laughed. "Are you kidding? And get scratched for my efforts? No, Defender won't understand, but that's why I stowed all my things in the wardrobe. No loose projectiles."

"Except for our bags," Henrik said, but he stood and placed his bag and cloak in the wardrobe along with Filip's before shutting it tight.

"Thanks guys," he said, cracking a yawn and closing his eyes. "Defender appreciates it, too."

"You're mental," Filip murmured, but he, too, used his belt and secured himself to his bed.

"Decided not to take any chances?" he teased.

"Hanging out with you is a chance all its own."

"What about you Henrik?" Christoffer asked. "Are you going to use a belt too?"

"*Err...*" he hesitated and then sighed, capitulating and getting his belt. "I'm going to regret this."

It must have been a premonition because warning bells again woke them in the dead of night. Secured as he was, Christoffer only felt the push and pull of gravity, sending him soaring and plummeting, as the ship crashed through the waters. Heartrate flying, he fumbled with the latch of the belt as Defender barked madly in terror, scrabbling for purchase nearby.

"I got you, boy," he said, grabbing a fistful of the border collie's collar. "You're safe. It's just a bunch of cranky whales."

"I hope it's whales, mate," Filip groused, rubbing his head where he'd knocked it getting out of bed. "Zar-Zar, Aleks, and the trolls can make quick work of them. I bet Bjarke can do it alone."

The bell tolled again – loud and resonant in the night, its clangor a groaning, groaning, groaning of disaster and danger and doom. It jarred the nerves and upset the stomach nearly as much as the swooping, plunging course of the ship as it clambered lugubriously through the ocean's high swells, struggling, struggling to find safe passage.

"It's not the same. It's rung differently," Henrik said worriedly, slipping on his boots.

The ship lurched and heaved, forcing them all to brace against the furniture and walls. Christoffer fought to keep Defender steady, but the border collie whined and yipped in fright, resisting his efforts. He lost his grip on the dog as the pealing took on a desperate tone.

A shivering, rumbling groan ran the length of the ship only to be broken by a sharp crack. The twanging of the bell shifted and lost its pitch. The floor tilted unnaturally and the door banged open in a burst of purple flames.

"Catch him," shouted Christoffer as Defender bolted for the door.

Zaria's hand shot out and snatched the dog by the collar. Pulling the frightened collie with her, she grabbed onto Filip's shirt with her other hand and hauled him close. When her boyfriend opened his mouth, she shook her head.

"No time to waste. We have to go topside, now," she said, fierce determination in her blazing violet eyes.

The air pressure changed and in a span of a breath they were gone. Something was desperately wrong and it wasn't whales, and it probably wasn't giants. More ominously still, the alarm bell had ceased ringing.

"Grab the bags," Henrik shouted, throwing wide the door to the wardrobe.

Christoffer caught his and Filip's, nearly fumbling them as the ship heaved up like something was trying to break it apart from beneath. The hairs on his arms rose heralding Zaria's return. She appeared in a misty shadow whose edges crackled with static and telltale purple light.

"What's happening?" Christoffer yelled, noticing that she was soaked to her skin, her hair plastered against her skull.

"You'll see," she said, not so reassuringly.

She gripped their shoulders so tightly her knuckles turned white. Air squeezed out of his lungs as she teleported them to the decking of the ship. They slammed into the wooden planks, bruising shins and knees as she misjudged the angle of the ship.

She scrambled to her feet quickly, missing Filip's outstretched hand. Instead, Christoffer grabbed it gratefully, and unsteadily climbed to his feet. All around them fear reigned supreme. The churning waves roared loudly in the night nearly drowning out their panicked shouts.

Water sloshed over the rails in a tidal wave, nearly sweeping Christoffer off his feet. As it was, retaining a grip on the bags was a feat in and of itself. Spotting the others, he immediately swapped the bags for Defender, thanking Geirr and hugging his madly barking dog close.

"I'll be back," Zaria said tightly, eyes strained with worry.

"Where are you going?" asked Filip.

"To see if there are others."

"I'll go too," he said, and when she made to protest, he raised an eyebrow in challenge.

"What's happening?" demanded Henrik, grabbing the rails as the ship tilted precariously and the creaking, groaning sound echoed again all around them.

Geirr looked spooked. "The ship's being torn apart."

"By what?" asked Filip.

But Christoffer knew, even without the river-trolls cursing like mad by the prow. The clamor and commotion tonight on the ship outstripped the frenetic organized furor from last night. Elves and ellefolken raced around like horses whipped into a froth and foam, eyes wide, terror leaking at the edges.

"Kraken," he stated woodenly, in shock.

His teasing earlier had only meant to be a joke not a premonition. No wonder his friends begged him not to make predictions or to taunt divine providence. He made a terrible prognosticator.

"Has it been spotted?" Henrik asked.

"Yes," Geirr confirmed, gazing at the blackened ocean, seeking the monster beneath the waves and spying a shadowy form, or what might have been one.

"Starboard," cried several voices and from the depths of the waves an unbelievably large meaty tentacle rose into the air.

"It's been a kraken good time knowing you all," Christoffer wheezed out as all the blood in his body seemed to freeze at the chilling sight.

It bothered him not one jot that nobody commented. Everyone's attention fixated in horrified awe on the point in the darkness where the tentacle rose. It curled menacingly toward the ship like a club ready to knock everyone topside into the seething sea.

"We need to go now," Zaria told Filip. "If you're still coming."

Utterly speechless, mouth agape, he gripped her shoulder and they zapped away, leaving the others behind.

"We need to help," Henrik said, snapping out of his fear-filled trance.

"Fire the harpoons," bellowed Bjarke as he helmed the ship, keeping her steady.

"Harpoons be matchsticks to this beast," snarled Olaf. "We not be making it out of here alive."

"Ye be a pessimistic fool," shouted Bjarke, eyes wild, but voice filled with conviction. "She not be prepared to take on two river-trolls. Lucky yer here."

Olaf grumbled something Christoffer couldn't hear as Aleks and Geirr dragged him away. They ran to nearby battle stations, their footfalls accompanied by sharp popping sounds that splintered the night air. At first Christoffer thought Zaria was returning with others she'd found below deck, but that was not the case. Humongous, oversized claws punched holes from below into the ship's deck like it was punching tissue paper, chunks of debris dangling off its limbs.

Defender fought him furiously, heaving against his restraining hold, trying to get away or fight. Christoffer forced him to stand still. No matter how brave, his little dog would be no match for a kraken on the hunt. He had no plans to give that sea monster a tasty snack.

"Why are there claws?" demanded Geirr, jumping out of the way as another one pierced the hull. "It has tentacles!"

"That tentacle is its tail," Henrik said, shoving ammo into the harpoon's loader and pivoting to aim.

"But the claws?" he pressed, loading a harpoon into the station Aleks manned with a sharp, aggravated click and slamming the panel closed.

"What do you think a kraken is?" asked the Stag Lord as he squinted down the sight and fired.

Christoffer held his breath watching the barbed spear fly through the night sky toward its target. He swallowed dryly when the meaty tentacle batted it away like a toothpick.

"Isn't it a monstrous squid? Octopus?" Aleks shouted. "It's what's on all the old sea maps."

"It's not that," Henrik said, firing again.

"What exactly is a kraken then?" demanded Geirr, suppressing a quiver in his voice.

As the claws retreated, ripping more of the ship apart, water flooded the space, burbling up from below like deadly lava. Henrik motioned to Geirr to prep another harpoon. He did, sliding it home with slightly trembling fingers. The Stag Lord pushed back his soaked bangs and looked them all dead in the eye. "A crab. It's a great big, massive, unbelievably huge crab."

"With a tail?" Aleks questioned, firing his harpoon once more into the night.

It sliced along the leading edge of the kraken's muscular tail, sending out a spray of blood and ichor.

"Nailed it!" cried Christoffer, just as a hideous screeching cry boiled up from below, curdling the waves like milk exposed to heat.

Defender barked madly beside him unable to withstand the high-pitched shriek. Covering their ears to block out the noise, they cringed as the sound drove shivers down their spines. Then everything turned eerily silent with the sea's frothing foam hissing and spitting out the last of its anger. An unnatural quiet filled the air. Christoffer and Geirr peered cautiously over the side, watching the waves settle.

"That was a close one," Geirr said, relieved.

"It's not over," warned Henrik, restocking his harpoon. "There's no way one little hit sends this beast back to its lair."

Aleks followed his lead. Wiping his brow, he asked again. "How does the kraken have a tail when it's a crab?"

"You know hermit crabs," the Stag Lord muttered. "They take on new shells when they outgrow their old ones. If the shell is too big, they wait for another crab to take it and discard its shell so they can take the smaller one."

"Yeah, so?" he asked. "Are you trying to tell me the kraken is a hermit crab?"

The ellefolken prince nodded. "One that grew too large to have a shell."

"How is that possible?" asked Christoffer, scanning the dark waters below.

"Where's its shell?" asked Geirr.

Henrik shrugged. "When it's this large, why does it need a shell?"

Shouts erupted on the deck followed by splashes. It was their only forewarning. The ship tilted as the claws came back and smashed into the side of the hull. Chunks of wood disintegrated under the kraken's brutal pounding. The railing they were holding was ripped out from under them. Geirr grabbed Christoffer's arm while Defender bit down on his shirt to keep him from falling overboard with the others.

"Me ship!" cried Bjarke in despair, tugging at his hair.

"Use my power," shouted Olaf, holding out his clawed hand.

The troll captain looked up in surprise, his mouth hanging open. "Are ye serious?"

"Just do it," snarled Olaf. "There be no time to dillydally. Be you wanting to live or not?"

Bjarke grabbed Olaf's hand and a colorless band of light immediately wrapped around their clasped hands.

Olaf's yellow eyes flared with magic and then Bjarke's, the glow as bright as any vehicle's headlamps. The waves churned and the boat slipped into the current's stream, listing drunkenly as it took on water. Round and round they went, faster and faster as the whirlpool picked up speed.

A space formed in the center of the maelstrom, widening as the waters pulled away. The kraken sunk like a stone, scrabbling for purchase, its mandibles clicking madly. Rolling on its back, its claws and legs clutched at the ship, but the rushing waters knocked its limbs away before it could get a bite into the ship's flanks.

Its screeching cry of rage shivered through the night like a lonely falcon. Its echo faded as the kraken fell further away from them toward the bottom of the ocean. The danger wasn't over, though, as the ship sunk lower in the cyclone. Many on board looked green around the gills, keeping good company with Geirr, as the ship went in ever tightening circles, spinning faster and faster.

"Watch out," cried Skorri from the skies above.

The kraken's tail suddenly gripped the ship's floating, dangling, anchor and tugged it down toward its shrieking, gloating, voracious mouth. Its outstretched maxillipeds, quivered eagerly, ready to snatch up its prize and swallow it whole. Several unfortunate crew met their fate and were swallowed down into the creature's depths.

"I'm never sailing again," moaned Geirr, turning away from the awful sight.

At nearly a ninety-degree angle to the ground, only their fading grip on the busted rail kept them from being swallowed whole.

Christoffer's arm wrapped around his loyal canine companion was no match for the struggling dog. Defender's eyes rolled wildly as vertigo hit and with a mighty shove, launched off Christoffer's stomach, pitching straight down.

"NO!" shouted Christoffer in shock, unable to save Defender.

"We got you," Zaria cried, as static discharge from her and Filip's sudden arrival swept across them like a blast of wind.

Defender halted mid-fall, surrounded by a purple glow. Christoffer wept in relief as she hauled him up and over the rail, while Filip did the same for Geirr. Defender floated up to them, legs scrambling madly in the air for purchase. Hugging him fiercely to his chest, and breathing in the musky wet dog smell at his nape, Christoffer breathed out a prayer of thanksgiving and felt his heartrate return from its galloping pace to a more normal range.

Together, Geirr and Filip swung Henrik over the rail while Zaria managed to get Aleks to safety. Laying on their stomachs, the view was no less terrifying as the ship was pulled closer and closer to the kraken. Christoffer took no chances with Defender and held him close with a death grip.

The trolls, which had started the deadly confrontation, focused their yellow eyes like a laser beam. Wind whipped their long hair around their heads. Flotsam and jetsam hurtled by in the water: harpoons, ropes, planks, crates, and broken masts. The mizzenmast, the largest of them all, angled down, turning at odds with the direction of the waters, controlled by magic.

"Abandon ship!" the river-trolls shouted as one. The crew dove for the maelstrom, heedless of its raging, grabbing at whatever they could find to stay afloat. Suddenly, the waters in the whirlpool fell away from under the kraken and Christoffer and the others went airborne against their will. Zaria's purple magic gathered them up and gravity did the rest.

The ship plunged into the kraken's gloating mouth; too late did it realize that its watery support was gone and it plunged shrieking to the ocean floor, sending up a plume of sand nearly as high as the whirlpool itself. Its cry died in its throat as the weight of its body and the height of its fall crushed its organs. It was over, the kraken was dead.

"I guess it really did need its shell," said Aleks, still a little shellshocked.

"Never leave home without it," Christoffer said sagely.

The river-trolls' glowing eyes faded and their floating bodies began to plummet.

"No," cried Zaria, throwing out a hand.

The diversion caused her magic hold on them to slip. With her supporting magic gone, they plummeted to join the kraken below.

Christoffer cried out, "Zaria, if you don't save us, I swear I will start kraken jokes! I'm not squidding about this!"

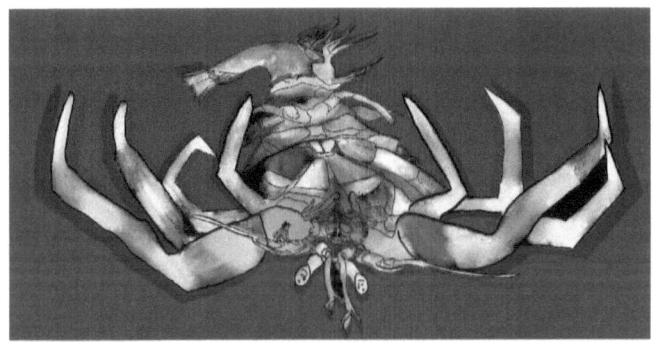

Chapter Three: The Svefnthorn

"Some threat. Aren't you always crackin' jokes?" she huffed, sweat pouring down her face as she juggled the seven of them with her magic. The trolls were nowhere to be seen.

"It worked though, didn't it?" he retorted, as his heartbeat slowed from another full out sprint. He wasn't sure how much more he could take on this deadly rollercoaster ride. Up. Down. Up. Down. No rails or tracks necessary.

"Where did Olaf and Bjarke go?" Aleks shouted over the rush and roar of the waters.

Christoffer angled his body around, enjoying the strange floating feeling now that he and his dog weren't about to be eaten or killed. "I don't see them."

"They must be around here somewhere," Filip said, trying unsuccessfully to maneuver his way closer to Zaria.

"How do you figure?" asked Geirr, frowning down at the lifeless body of the kraken far below.

The large crustacean looked like a darkened smudge on the otherwise white sandy floor. If anyone else was down there they weren't moving.

"The whirlpool," Zaria said, reaching out with her fingers to glide them in the swirling waters. "It's still active."

"Do you think it behaves similarly to the one in Olaf's river?" asked Aleks.

"One way to find out," Christoffer said. Grabbing the fey king's arm, he leveraged himself and Defender across the space. Floating toward the inner rim of the maelstrom, it wasn't until he was nearly beside it that they understood what he meant to do.

"Christoffer, no!" shouted Zaria.

"It's okay," he said, pushing his hands and then arms into the swift-moving current. "It'll be okay."

"How do you know?" she cried out, purple eyes glinting with worry.

"Because," he said, taking a deep breath. "All of the crew are gone."

Gently pushing Defender into the water, he used the collie's momentum to fully submerge as well. Circling downwards into the violent maelstrom, Christoffer held Defender close to keep him from sticking his head out as if they were in a car ride. The two were sucked down and away, whipping through the spinning waters. With each passing turn the blurry faces of his friends got smaller, but whether by proximity or magic he heard them fret about the crazy stunt he'd pulled.

"Well, that's just perfect," grumbled Geirr, throwing his hands into the air. "What does he expect us to do, follow him?"

"I'm not following," squawked Skorri.

Filip flipped onto his back and stared at the two circling white ravens. "We'll meet you on the shore."

"Airi you follow," Aleks commanded. "Keep an eye on that one. We'll find you soon."

Then with a little guidance from Zaria's magic they formed a human chain and sunk one by one into the whirlpool falling away after him. Down and down and down and down. Down and down.

"And when it stops nobody knows," he mused.

It was as if the magic was waiting for him to say that because all of a sudden, he was spat out like a giant turd-shaped sea cucumber, in one great squelching go. Split seconds later his friends reemerged one right after the other leaving Christoffer to conclude that the whirlpool's rotation must've sped up drastically.

They were soaked to the skin, but Christoffer supposed they were before the watery transport to the ocean floor, so that didn't make much difference in the grand scheme of things. The ocean floor – though covered in white sand – was dark in the shadows cast by the maelstrom towering high above. From below, its sheer height was an unfathomable experience. How had the trolls managed to move that much water? The volume of it was astronomical.

The whirlpool moved like it was alive. It hissed and spit and roared and moaned above them, and yet, it was strangely quiet there in the middle of its eye. Not tranquil; too much chaos battered and battled around them for it to be tranquil. Subdued, maybe, hushed. Like the sound was held at a distance from them.

The kraken's mangled body lay as a heap on the floor. A mountain too big to climb, its graying flesh gross and slick with mucus. Down here it smelled stale, airless, which made perfect sense since it was the bottom of the ocean. The looming mass of water shifted above them and Christoffer covered his nose as a rotten-egg smell hit him. Its source couldn't be the kraken; the creature was freshly killed.

"That stench is awful," complained Filip. "Is it the kraken?"

"It's your butt kraken," joked Christoffer.

"It's your fart kraken," Filip shot back petulantly, causing him to laugh in delight and Defender to bark.

"Can't be any of those things. It hasn't even had a chance to start decaying. Too soon," Aleks said, echoing Christoffer's earlier thoughts.

"Something is foul down here," Geirr insisted.

"That's just the smell of the ocean, I think," said Zaria, walking gingerly around the kraken, examining it.

"The ocean never smells like this," Filip denied.

"Yeah, sure, not on the surface," she agreed. "Not unless there's rotting seaweed or exploding plankton or something."

"Exploding plankton?" questioned Christoffer with a raised eyebrow.

"It's a thing," Zaria defended.

"Sure, sure," he agreed, making a crazy symbol to the others.

Zaria rolled her eyes and walked over to Henrik. The Stag Lord stood stoically beside the beast, either not bothered by the smell, or a very good actor. He and Aleks took opposite sides of the sea monster and together they scanned for their missing trolden companions. No signs of life greeted them. The ocean waters were dark as midnight, and if life hid in them, it did not reveal itself to the group.

"I see a light," said Zaria suddenly, pointing into the blackened depths.

Christoffer saw it, too, but his experience with the mermaids from hell made him leery to seek out the source of that light. Creatures of the ocean depths used light to lure in unsuspecting prey. Filip and Aleks had similar concerns, guessing by the expressions exchanged between them.

"How can we tell if it's friendly?" asked Filip.

"I can make another submersible," Zaria suggested.

Henrik nodded, liking the idea. "That's a good idea, but before we go, we must first salvage something from this fellow."

"We're harvesting body parts from the kraken?" Geirr asked, aghast. The look of disgust returned as his nose twitched in dismay.

"Oh, like a trophy? To show others we killed it?" asked Christoffer.

"No to both of those, and we didn't kill it," Henrik said. "The river-trolls did."

"Then what do you mean?" Zaria asked. "Why do we want to harvest it?"

"The witch of the woods," Aleks hinted meaningfully.

"Oh, right," Geirr said, somewhat relieved. "We need to bring her back the first two things we collect."

"Pity she never told us what exactly it was we were meant to collect," Zaria said. "She's crafty, the witch."

"Better than seashells," Christoffer said.

"Well, mate," Filip said on a low whistle. "This is more exciting for our gather quest. It's definitely not a shell." Scratching his head, he looked at them and the kraken meaningfully. "So... what do we take back to her? I don't think our weapons can carve anything off this thing. It's more massive than a mountain. You'd need a blade the size of a whale to hack this sucker up."

Henrik shrugged. "I've no idea. My father and grandfathers never mentioned this."

"What? No, kraken seafood boil or chowder recipes in your family cookbooks?" Christoffer teased.

"None," he said soberly. "They're so rarely seen that even we can forget they're not myths."

"True, true," Christoffer agreed. "Even Olaf scoffed at the idea of one not too long ago."

"I bet he's eating his words now," muttered Geirr.

"Only if we bring him back some crab legs," he quipped, earning some groans from the group.

"Well, I'm pretty certain crab legs were not what the witch was after," Zaria said, bringing them back on track. She circled around again, more slowly, peering intently at the sea monster's bloated body. "It really is disgusting, like a slug meets an alien."

"Oh, now that you said it, I can totally picture baby krakens attacking faces," Filip said. He shuddered. "I kind of wish I hadn't thought of it, though."

"I miss Vingar," Aleks said. "If we're in need of mythical sea creatures I would take him any day. His help in Niffleheim saved me."

"Saved us, mate. All of us," Filip said.

Christoffer approached the head with its black, sightless eyes and rigid, outstretched maxillipeds. He could almost imagine it shivering back to life. The hairs on the back of his neck rose at the thought. He held Defender closer, ignoring the dog's protesting whine.

Looking hastily away from its mouth, he meant to move on, but... Freezing in place as his mind caught up with his eyes, Christoffer mentally re-examined what he'd just seen. Turning back, he peered into the giant mouth and there stuck on a mandible, wedged as if waiting for them to find, lay a treasure that Christoffer was sure the witch would want.

"I think I found it," he told the others eagerly. "Someone grab Defender."

Filip took the border collie, and Christoffer nodded his thanks. Reaching out to grasp the kraken's gray drying flesh, he hauled himself up onto its outstretched form.

"Be careful," Zaria warned, picking her way over the seabed to him.

"What did you find?" Aleks asked, coming over and looking up at the giant crab.

Climbing carefully, tucking his feet into various pits and pocks in the crab's flesh, he dragged himself skyward. Pointing, he said, "It's got a shield wedged like a popcorn shuck in its mouth."

"A shield?" Geirr said dubiously. "Wouldn't that have been crushed?"

Filip cupped his mouth and shouted, "How old is the shield?"

"How should I know?" Christoffer complained. "I haven't got it yet."

"Is it shiny?" Zaria asked.

He gave her an incredulous look. "It's covered in mucus or something."

"Ew," she said, lip curling. "I am glad you're getting it and not me."

"Same," agreed Geirr from the sidelines, touching his salt-encrusted clothes with a grimace.

Christoffer laughed and scrambled the rest of the way up the kraken's body. Jumping to one of the broken and brittle maxillipeds, he clung to the massive tentacle-like body part and swung himself up. Precariously perched on top, he leaned forward and scooted up higher still.

Once, as he neared the top his foot slipped when the mandible broke beneath his weight. He lost purchase and nearly toppled to the ground. "Whoa!" he cried out, feet flailing, seeking something to grip.

Quick reflexes saved him; well, that and a bit of a magical boost from the resident sorceress in the group. Zaria bit her lip, and Christoffer could tell she wished to scold him for his inattention to the task at hand. Lucky for him she refrained and with her help, he no longer dangled by one hand on a mucus-and-saltwater covered appendage.

Taking great care, and being precise with his movements Christoffer started the uphill climb again. Creaking echoed through the kraken's lifeless form. He paused, holding his breath, waiting to see if it could bear his weight. Only when the shivering sounds ceased and the tremors stopped, did he move again, testing each handhold before trusting it with his weight. Transitioning at the creature's mandibles, he hopped onto the sturdier limb.

Close enough now to see the shield, Christoffer could make out that it once had an elaborate pattern. Time and wear eroded the design but he could see the remnants of runes scratched into the surface. Grabbing hold of the shield with both hands, he pulled. The shield held in place, wedged firmly in the kraken's mouth.

"Be careful, mate," warned Filip.

"Gee, thanks," he said. "I was really aiming for reckless endangerment, you know?"

"This is no time for jokes," Henrik said, frowning. He held his hand out, palm up. "We need to get that shield and get moving. Now."

"What is it?" asked Geirr.

"There's more rainfall," said Henrik. "I fear the maelstrom is imminently close to collapsing."

Zaria glanced at the turbulent waters around them. "I don't think I can hold it back if the trolls' magic fails."

"Quit distracting me, then," Christoffer said. "I got a shield to fetch."

Turning back to the stuck shield, he rubbed his palms together and laid hands on it. Tugging with all his might, he grunted and managed to budge the shield a tiny bit. The slimy coating did not make for an easy grip. Deciding to work with the unctuous substance, he brushed the shield, pushing the slime down into the mandible's joint.

"What are you doing?" asked Aleks. "Stop wasting time!"

"I'm lubricating the sucker," Christoffer retorted. "You try budging this thing otherwise. The sword in the stone wasn't held this fast."

Wiggling the shield back and forth, Christoffer gently worked. Inch by inch the shield loosened. The juncture of the mandible worked itself open and freed the prize. Seizing the shield, Christoffer raised it above his head in victory, crying, "Got it!"

"Hurry and get down here," Filip called out.

He hadn't noticed while working on freeing his treasure, but the whirlpool did seem on the verge of collapsing. The column of swirling water weaved back and forth drunkenly, its shape wavering and shrinking. Water pelted them like hail, hard and cold, stinging wherever it landed.

Christoffer leapt down, heedless of his footing, eager to reach his friends on the ground. By the time he got to them Zaria had built a clear, bubble-shaped submersible. He could already make out Defender inside it, running around and sniffing at the seats. The others were scrambling through the hatchway, a tangle of limbs pushing and pulling each other into safety.

As he neared, Henrik held out his hand and Christoffer grabbed it. Pulled inside, he was pushed into a seat and a harness – new to Zaria's submersible design specs – snapped in place around his torso. "Good thinking," he murmured as Henrik took the empty space beside him and buckled up.

Geirr slammed the hatch shut not a moment too soon as the waters above them buckled inward, collapsing and rushing to fill the void. Darkness poured over them like liquid ink and the little sub lifted in the rising waters. A premonition, an inkling of a thought, sprung to mind and Christoffer snatched up Defender and held the startled dog close to his chest, arms locking into place holding him still.

The submersible tumbled and flailed through the shifting currents and pressure. His ears popped. His eyes strained to see. His body jerked against the restraint as they were flipped end over end. Defender yipped and Geirr made retching sounds in the dark, but the plighted teen had nothing left to give after the night's adventures. The craft was pushed by unseen streams and currents, probably propelled by Zaria's magic, away from the danger.

When the ride evened out, she began lifting them skyward. Fish curious to the source of her light darted in and out of sight, shining like pieces of purple and silver glass as they flashed to and fro. Ahead, the waters grew brighter by degrees until the sun's rays did more than permeate, and actually sent down bright shafts of light into the sea. Following one up they breeched the surface like a whale, landing with a plop and a huge splash, sending out a plume of water.

There, bobbing like a buoy in the early morning sun, Christoffer finally felt like they were out of danger. He wasn't the only one. Collectively, they all sighed in relief, breathing deeply for the first time in what seemed hours, and not just because the sulfur smell was gone.

With danger behind them, his friends turned their eyes to the prize he'd found on the kraken.

"May I see it?" asked Henrik, holding out his hand.

Christoffer passed it to the Stag Lord. He turned it over in his hands, wiping ineffectively at the grime that coated the shield. The sludge clung like barnacles to a whale's skin, refusing to budge, instead smearing. Angling it away from him, Henrik squinted in an attempt to bring the runes into focus.

"I can't be sure because of the state of the shield, but I think it's a svefnthorn."

"A svefnthorn?" Zaria asked, leaning over and peering closer at it.

"A sleep thorn," he explained, handing it to her. "It would explain why we haven't seen the kraken in over a thousand years."

Christoffer grinned. "It's magic? Tell me it's magic."

Henrik nodded. "It's magic."

"Very powerful since it put the kraken to sleep," Aleks guessed.

Filip frowned, disturbed by a thought. "The svefnthorn was still lodged in the kraken's mouth. Did it's magic finally fade out? Or worse, did something wake it up? What is capable of overriding the power of the shield?"

"We already know the answer to that," said Henrik. "It's why Olaf is trying to gather allies; it's why we're trying to fix the sw—err—thingy."

"A dragon," Christoffer supplied.

"When is the answer not a dragon?" Geirr said dryly.

He rubbed his hands together in glee. "Ooo, a riddle. Let me think… when is the answer not a dragon? When it's a kraken? A draken? A kragon?"

"We need to find the river-trolls," Aleks said, interrupting. "That's our next goal. Find them and get to shore."

"Shore might be easier," Zaria remarked, pointing through the clear side of the submersible to a spit of land sprung from the sea like a safe haven after the rough night.

"Land ho!" cried Christoffer.

Geirr grinned, pumping his fist in the air. "Land ho!"

"Awhooo!" howled Defender, tail wagging.

With a thought, Zaria directed their watercraft to the shore. They beached, the bottom of the submersible plowing through the sand, slowing and then stopping. The hatch was opened and they all stumbled out.

Before them the soft sands stretched out like a bridal veil, white and lacy. Above them, signs of civilization sped by on a windy road. Some vehicles were starting to park a little way off and beachgoers were unpacking trunks and coolers.

Aleks and Zaria shared a silent look. Then at a subtle flick of her hand, the little clear submersible melted like mist back into the ocean, disappearing with an outgoing wave. Filip handed Christoffer's backpack to him and he slipped it on over his shoulders. A short whistle called Defender to heel and the group of them trudged up to the road.

Plunging back into the modern world, far from the realm of enchanted Norway was a shock to the system; like suddenly finding oneself in a foreign land where others looked different and spoke a different language. He knew he should recognize it, but the world felt off-kilter... and not just from their most recent tumbleweed experience in the depths of the ocean.

"This feels surreal," he told the others.

Filip pushed back his bangs and surveyed the gathering early morning crowds, eager to take in the good weather and sunshine. "It's bizarre that they're moving around, too, since we activated the stargazer, but then again, we don't usually run into people after we leave Fredrikstad."

"The stargazer's magic is only so strong," Aleks reminded. "It allows us to escape the city without our parents or others noticing. It doesn't freeze the whole country in its tracks."

"We know, we know," Christoffer said mildly, waving away his words. "It's just weird."

At the road, Zaria motioned everyone close around her. She glanced this way and that, peering over their shoulders, checking for witnesses. Seeing none, she conjured into existence six bikes, pretending to pull each one from a clump of overgrown bushes. One by one they mounted them and fell into their natural ranks behind Aleks.

"Where are we headed, mate?" asked Filip.

Aleks tapped his temple. "Not sure yet, just following the map in my head."

"We should look for a bridge," Henrik advised, calling from the back of the group.

"How come?" asked Geirr, looking over his shoulder.

"Where else will we find a pair of river-trolls?" Christoffer bantered with a knowing grin, keeping an eye on Defender as he trotted alongside in the grass.

"Oh, of course," said Zaria, laughing. "Bridges and trolls. Isn't that where all of this started?"

"Fitting, then, that it comes full circle," Christoffer said.

"Again," Henrik said.

"Don't make it sound too ominous," warned Christoffer. "Or the others will bite your head off."

Chapter Four: It's Troll, Not Toll, Bridge

They rode for several hours while the morning grew brighter and the sun blazed hot overhead. The coastal road took them in and out of several populated areas. For once, they stopped at a restaurant for food instead of bumming magical meals from Zaria. Defender drank greedily from a water bowl the restaurant owner had thoughtfully provided.

Sitting there with his friends, Christoffer could just as easily have been a university student and not a kid playing hooky. Amongst the normal hustle and bustle, he was as far removed from the kraken attack and dragons as if he was on the moon. It felt wrong.

The long hours on the bike passed for an adventure, but not the magical enchanting one he'd wanted. This was a grind. He was tired and sore and very much in need of a saddle and a bear. Magical travel was definitely a cut above pedaling.

Defender, lucky dog, rode in a little wagon Zaria had conjured after he got worn out from running and exploring. His added weight made every hill steeper. Christoffer's calves ached from the workout, but he didn't complain; well, at least not about Defender being with him on the trip.

"I hate to be a broken record –" he started.

"But are we there yet?" finished Filip. "My butt is going numb."

Zaria winced and nodded. "These seats are not the comfiest."

"Yeah, I'm missing the polar bears," Christoffer said.

"Or bears in general," said Geirr.

"I'm missing Norwick," said Henrik.

Christoffer's eyes lit up. "Yes, winter-wyverns. Let's ride those! We'll get where we're going so much faster than on these bikes. No offense, Zaria."

"We're not far now," Aleks said, scouting ahead.

"You've said that before," he whined. "Seriously, I think you tell me that so I keep going."

Aleks smirked a little but said nothing. He slowed at an upcoming fork in the road and everyone braked with him. Closing his eyes, the fey king focused on a map only he could see. Fingering his raven-motif cuff, he glanced skyward at the darkening clouds heralding rain. "I don't think we'll beat the rain."

"Which way do we go?" asked Zaria.

"That way," he said, pointing north. They began pedaling once more.

Christoffer pouted. "No winter-wyverns then? Are you sure? If we're above the clouds we wouldn't care if it rained or not."

"You'd care," Geirr assured him, passing him in the lineup. "You'd be colder, wetter, and more miserable up in the sky if it rained."

"Oh sure, bring logic into this. We've got a sorceress, what care we for trivial things?"

"I'm not a weatherman."

"You could be!" he singsonged, causing her to chuckle and shake her head. "You just haven't tried."

"Christoffer," she warned.

"Zaria," he countered lightly. "You weren't sure about teleporting either, but once you tried it you found it wasn't half bad."

She bit her lip. "That's fair."

"So don't you think you ought to try the magic before you say no to the magic?" he cajoled, pressing his advantage and giving her a winning smile.

"I don't know," she hedged, looking uncertain.

"At least try," he urged. "How about something that's like your fireballs? Elemental? Maybe wind? Or maybe water? You've seen what Bjarke and Olaf did with both to create the maelstrom."

"When did you get to be so persuasive?" she asked.

"I rolled a natural twenty," he told her, laughing. Defender barked in agreement, tail wagging at the playful banter.

"You must've," she said, shaking her head, amused. The fact she got his D&D joke made him proud, like a mama bird watching her chick grow up.

As the clouds broke, sending down a cool shower of rain, he glanced at her meaningfully. Zaria squinted hard, concentrating. She didn't need any outward sign to perform magic, but sometimes, especially when learning new aspects of her magical ability, she made gestures or facial expressions.

A few moments later a soft breeze blew against Christoffer's face. He couldn't tell whether the breeze was magical or not, and judging by Zaria's mystified expression, she didn't know either. The wind sighed away as quickly as it had come.

"You don't have to get it on your first attempt," he reminded her. "Perhaps you can try to make the rain stop or more intense? Or even try to make a projectile, like a water ball instead of a fireball?"

"I suppose we're already soaked," she murmured, and taking her hand off the handlebar of her bike formed a globular ball made of water.

"Oh no," Christoffer cried out, seeing where this was heading by her mischievous grin. Pedaling faster, he pulled ahead and the water ball splashed loudly against the pavement. The whoosh sounds of the water exploding woke Defender who immediately clambered out of the wagon and stayed far back from their antics.

"Hold still," she teased, forming another projectile.

"Filip, save me," he called out, passing on the side, trying to use her boyfriend as a shield.

"What's going on?" he asked, unaware of the incoming missile. It landed with a slap against the side of his neck, exploding upwards. "Whoa!" he shouted, bike spinning out of control.

"Oh no!" Zaria shouted, flinging out a hand. She steadied his bike with a touch of magic before she could grip the handlebar and steer. "I'm so, so sorry Filip. I was aiming for Christoffer."

He wiped his face with his shirtsleeve and grinned at her. "New powers? That's cool, Zar-Zar!"

"You're too nice," she said, fretting over the red mark her water ball had caused. "Does it sting?"

"A little, but not like a sting from a fireball." At her shocked look, he added, "You know, from a dragon?"

Her face relaxed. She touched the side of his neck. "Still, I didn't mean to hurt you."

"Oh sure, sure, so you just wanted to hurt me. I see how it is," Christoffer complained.

"You wanted me to try something new. You volunteered to be the test subject."

"I don't remember saying that, do you remember me saying that?" he joked, posing the question to Filip.

"Not sure what you mean. I heard you volunteer, mate," Filip said with a straight face.

"*Et tu*, Brute?"

Zaria formed another water ball and lobbed it at him. Christoffer ducked, hunching his shoulders, and peddled faster. Passing Geirr for added safety and extra distance from his sorceress friend, he thought he was out of her reach.

"I heard you, too," said Geirr, smirking and slowing down so Zaria could pass him, too.

"Hey! No fair!" he shouted, raising off his seat to try to gain momentum and speed.

"Must've been the wind," consoled Henrik, letting Christoffer change positions with him in the lineup.

"Thank you, Henrik," Christoffer said gratefully. He turned a stink eye on the others. "At least someone is on my side."

"Your powers are expanding," remarked Henrik, waving Zaria ahead of him, too. "The rain and wind are interfering with your aim. Try to compensate for them if you can."

"I'm surrounded by a bunch of traitors," Christoffer bemoaned, but grinned widely and darted back and forth avoiding globs of water being thrown at him.

They splattered against the pavement sending spray upward, soaking his legs and jeans. Pedaling hard and leaning into the handlebars he aligned himself behind

Aleks, riding in his draft. The fey king raised an eyebrow in his direction and applied the brakes.

"Oh no, you don't," he said, smirking as Christoffer flew by.

An explosion of water ricocheted under his tires. He barely hung onto the handlebars and kept his balance. "She's a maniac!"

Zaria chortled and the sound made him wince. Christoffer knew that laugh. Glancing behind him, his eyes widened as the sorceress princess hurled a perfectly aimed water ball at his face. It splashed with enough force to knock him off his bike. Nimble reflexes saved him from an ignominious ending. Spluttering, he wiped his face as best he could under the rain and cleared his eyes. Hands up, he shouted, "I surrender. I surrender."

Giggling at his antics, she hopped off the bike and gave him a one-armed hug. "That'll teach you," she teased.

"Yeah," he said. "It'll teach me not to open my big fat mouth. You mastered those water projectiles fast."

She shrugged nonchalantly, but her bashful appearance soon gave way to bright happiness. "I did, didn't I? I wonder if I can do similar things with the other elements."

He grinned. "I'd suggest lightning, but I don't want to get fried. How about Filip volunteer for that one?"

Filip snorted. "Oh no, I don't think I'll volunteer for that one."

"Volunteer, volun-told, same difference, right?" Christoffer asked the others.

Geirr smirked. "Filip's already electrocuted by the magical bolt of young love, what's one more bolt to the heart?"

The sun broke out from behind a cloud, and the rain soon slowed into a sun shower. The air turned just the slightest bit stagnant and muggy as the sudden storm petered out. Christoffer plopped onto the grass beside the road to stretch his legs and catch a breather. Defender laid beside him and promptly started snoring. It was hard work to train a sorceress and escape a water attack.

While everyone rested and dried off under Zaria's wind tunnel magic, Henrik and Aleks consulted a compass and one of her maps. There was a brief argument about the best way to go, but Henrik conceded the navigation to Aleks when he was reminded that it wasn't about getting to a specific place, but instead finding specific people.

"Who knew a couple of river-trolls would be so difficult to find?" Filip said, his head resting in Zaria's lap as she ran her fingers through his hair.

Geirr shrugged. "How many bridges are there? Too many to count I suppose."

"We're nearly there," Aleks reassured. "I can sense it. The map is a little vague, but I know we're headed in the right direction. We'll find them soon."

"I swear you just said that," Christoffer said with a small huff.

Zaria shifted and she and Filip climbed to their feet. Grasping her handlebars she said to him, "Come on lazy bones, let's get to riding."

"Can you just conjure a car? Or maybe a ride?"

Everyone laughed, including Aleks. With renewed energy they cycled on into the late afternoon. Zaria refreshed them with water, sports drinks, energy bars, and sandwiches along the way. The short distance Aleks had promised grew uncomfortably long. Even he began slowing down. The day was reaching its end and it seemed they were no closer to their goal.

"Is your mental map on the fritz again?" Geirr asked, gliding to a stop. "We've been at this all day."

"I didn't want to say anything," Filip added, looking relieved that Geirr had brought it up first.

Aleks frowned into the distance, his sweaty red hair plastered against his face. "It's working, but –"

"But?" Zaria prodded.

"But," he continued slowly, sounding it out. "I think they're moving."

"Why?" asked Geirr.

"They're on a river," Henrik answered. "They must be traversing the Efjorden."

"Where are they heading?"

"To the Eford Bridges," Henrik said.

"We're close," Aleks promised. "We don't even have to backtrack."

"That's good," said Christoffer, "Or we might have to cause you bodily harm."

Geirr cracked a wry grin. "Can you give me an exact figure? How far is close?"

"Closer than before," the fey king said enigmatically.

"One good goose egg from Airi," swore Christoffer. "Just see if I don't ask her to knock you on your forehead when I see her."

"Woof," agreed a sleepy Defender.

"What are you complaining about? You got to ride most of the day," Christoffer grumbled. "Spoiled dog. You don't know how good you have it."

With a fixed destination, their progress sped up like a bloodhound on the scent. Aleks stopped meandering along winding roads and paths and took them straight as an arrow to the bridges. Sunlight gilded the bridges as if it were melted butter, triggering hunger pangs from starving stomachs.

"I'm ready for a hot bath and a good meal," Filip said, gazing at the first of the bridges before them.

"Count me in," said Christoffer. "I'll take the same."

"Which bridge?" asked Zaria tiredly from the back. She'd been flagging the last hour.

Filip wrapped an arm around her shoulders. "My guess is the first one."

"That's optimistic of you," said Geirr. "I bet it's the last one."

"Shh," the blond teen warned, glancing pointedly at his wilting girlfriend. "She's beat. If the trolls had any sense of decency, they would pick the first bridge."

"No matter which bridge it is, we're at the end," Henrik encouraged. "Let's go together."

They rode abreast; the road was free of cars at this time of day. As they crossed the first bridge, the wind rose, ruffling hair and clothes like a mother at her child's return. Reaching the first island, sheltered by the trees, the group paused to look back. No figure waited on the bridge.

"Not the first bridge then," said Henrik, before turning his gaze to the smallest of the three bridges.

"Perhaps it's this one?" ventured Filip. "What do you think, mate? What are the chances?"

A shrill cry split the air as a white raven swooped down from above. Aleks grinned, holding out an arm for Airi and said, "I think they're very good."

"You found me," she cooed, knocking low in her throat and nuzzling against his hand.

"I will always find you, girl," he said. "You can count on that."

"Eye-riii!" she trilled, fluffing out her feathers and preening. "I told you. I told you. Master is smart. He finds anything. He finds us fast."

Aleks' grin stretched wider. "Airi, your talking is improved! How can you say I'm the smartest? You're the smartest, cleverest, girl."

"I know," she said with a little chirrup.

"*Harrumph,*" came a sour Skorri from his perch high in the trees. "It is lucky you arrived. I was planning to leave you and return to my master."

One white raven is a sight to behold, but seeing two in such close proximity is extremely unusual. Rare already, the white ravens hold a special place in the enchanting worlds of myth and fable and are highly sought after for their loyalty, ability to hold secrets, talk and deliver messages.

Airi came to Aleks on her own and bonded to him. Skorri they had won – at least the right to introduce him to another – after the raven had agreed to a bet. The bird was still sore about losing, but Christoffer didn't think he would renege on a bet, as his honor and that of his former master's was on the line.

"I think you're relieved we found you," Zaria told the raven.

Skorri grunted, eyeing them warily from above and said nothing. His obstinate refusal to agree with them tickled Christoffer's funny bone. He no longer felt the bird a pest, but rather a source of entertainment. Cantankerous and sarcastic though he may be, the raven was loyal and honorable and willing to find a source of new happiness with his old master's transformation back into rock and mountain.

"Shall we go on?" pressed Henrik and they all kicked off the ground and took off for the next bridge.

Before the first tire made it a quarter of the way across, a large misshapen figure appeared at the midpoint of the bridge. Fog and mist seemed to roll from it, but neither Christoffer nor the others stopped. They rushed forward, ditching bikes hither and yon on the road. Everyone spoke at once and nobody heard anything anyone said in the cacophony of greetings.

Olaf separated from Bjarke, letting go of the portly troll's support to stand on his own. The river-troll's haggard appearance was apparent despite the fresh change of clothes. He had neither energy nor verve. His scales shone a dull beige and steel, lacking vibrancy and depth of color, as if he'd dried out. His long fur, though clean, limped along. His gnarled hands were bandaged all over, with barely a knuckle peeping out.

"The magic you two did was amazing to behold," Zaria said, reaching out a comforting hand to the older troll. "How are you holding up? How is the Glomma?"

"If the dragon knows about what be happening with the kraken, he not yet be pressing his advantage. Princess, the Glomma be safe."

"For now," intoned Bjarke darkly.

"What do you mean?" asked Aleks.

"His reserves are wiped out," said the troll captain. He looked to Olaf with a new sense of admiration and respect. "I did not expect ye to give me everything ye had left."

Olaf waved it away. "Time and recuperation will be returning it."

"Time ye do not have," Bjarke said speculatively, eyeing his cousin. "Not while ye need to be gaining allies and a dragon encroaches on yer borders. Ye can't be in two places at once."

"Be you willing to be Olaf's second head?" asked Olaf.

Bjarke watched the waters for a time, before giving a reluctant nod. "It be owed to ye."

Olaf's gaze turned sympathetic. "I not be needing you to be my second forever."

"It will feel like it," the troll captain said, despondent.

"Be you able to bear it?"

"I must, or the sacrifice ye made be in vain," Bjarke said, mustering some life. "Besides, there is no heir to the ellefolken."

Christoffer and the others nodded to Henrik, causing him to blush. "There's not – that is to say, I –"

"We not be blaming you," said Olaf, hastily. "It be beyond your control."

"Aye," Bjarke agreed, nodding. "The dragon's activity is not your doing, and your father just became king."

"It not being the time for the Princeling to sacrifice."

As the sun hung low behind him, haloing him in bright gold, Bjarke proclaimed, "It be mine. I will be yer second head."

As soon as the words left his mouth, sunlight blazed bright, casting him in rays of amber light. Christoffer squinted and looked away. The sound of water rushing filled his ears. Water from the fjord rose in a column and raced toward the trolls. It encased their bare feet and climbed up their legs and torso with frightening speed.

The water wrapped around them forming a liquid chrysalis, drawing them nearer to each other. The river-trolls stepped closer, Bjarke hugging Olaf's unsteady form. Heads tipped back, necks strained, they gasped for air as the water covered their faces, their long noses the last things to submerge.

Everyone held their breath as the waters swirled around them, frosting at the edges, but never freezing fully. Their blurred outline shifted restlessly inside the cocoon like a strange pulsating boneless thing. Then with a crack, the icy edges crashed, and it all came splashing down.

Chapter Five: The Two-Headed Troll

The waters receded as fast as they had arrived, slipping back into the fjord like a silent specter, for nobody paid them any mind, too focused on the figure before them. Christoffer got his first glance at the river-trolls he thought he knew without the icy water covering and hiding their shape. They were foreign and yet indisputably recognizable.

The large, lumpy shape was clearly a river-troll, and emerging from it were two distinct heads, one Olaf and the other Bjarke. Both shared one torso, four arms, and two legs. No tails obviously, as only mountain-trolls had tails. One of the hands scratched at its neck, pushing aside some coarse cloth, and Christoffer saw a rough, red scar bisecting the troll's body straight between the two halves.

"Olaf? Bjarke?" Zaria asked, confused, reaching toward them to take a hand, but hesitating, unsure what to do.

Their heads turned as one to her, twin sets of bright yellow eyes peering at her quizzically as if trying to remember who she was. As the light of recognition dawned, they said as one, their voices overlapping, "We be called Olebjørn."

"Olebjørn," she said slowly, caution lacing every word. "Do you remember us?"

The right head, Bjarke, laughed deep belly-filled laughs. "Of course we do, Princess."

She breathed a sigh of relief. "I am glad, but I don't understand how becoming a two-headed troll helps Olaf. His goals were different from Bjarke's."

"Follow Olebjørn, little Princess," said Olaf, the left head. "Ye shall see."

They stretched out two hands, both from Olaf's side and Zaria tentatively held the lower of the two. A whirlpool opened beneath the bridge and she and the two-headed troll jumped into it. Filip and Henrik jumped next and Christoffer and Defender followed with Geirr and Aleks on their heels.

Airi was reluctant to let her master go so soon after finding him again and so he took her with him. Skorri squawked in annoyance, but swooped down after them before the pool closed over their heads and the waters settled, hiding their passage. The ravens protested the whole ride down, fretting about getting wet.

Sliding down and down, and around and around, Christoffer landed with a soft swoosh into Olaf's dining room next to the others. Airi and Skorri tumbled out, bedraggled and cranky. Shaking their feathers, they flew to various perches – Airi to Aleks' shoulder and Skorri to Henrik's.

"Where is your cloak?" demanded the cross raven.

Henrik sighed ruefully and hunkered down, slinging his backpack off his shoulder. "I'll unpack it."

The minute he'd draped it around his shoulders Skorri settled in its golden antlers. Henrik rolled his eyes at the plight of his mantle. Something about its towering shape and shiny, golden sheen attracted the ravens. Even Airi eyed one of the long tines but decided she missed Aleks more and stayed put.

Christoffer whistled, turning on his heel and taking in the space. The ankle-deep wintry slush of water and ice was gone. The strange humidity in the room had disappeared. But most surprising of all, what had been melting furniture was no longer malformed heaps of ice. Glittering icy surfaces with intricate runic carvings shone out at him everywhere he looked. Counters, stools, tables, and chairs decorated the space like the dining room of a cruise ship.

Many of the seats were filled with the castaways from *Ursula*. Spying Phoebe at one of the tables, he waved, relief suffusing him. She'd not been one of the unlucky few who fell overboard before the trolls had jointly taken out the kraken. Phoebe waved back, grinning and returned to chatting with her companions. She paused suddenly and did an about face to stare at her captain, her mouth agape.

"Oy! Captain! You gained a second head and enough limbs to be a squid!"

Chatter halted as the whole room focused on the two-headed troll in their midst. Olebjørn waved them off with a hearty, "Quit yer gawking. Ye all be acting like ye never be seeing a two-headed troll before."

"We haven't!" Phoebe called back.

"Well, now ye can say ye did," they said gruffly.

"But why did you join?" she pressed. "The kraken's already gone."

Cheers rose up amongst the crowd. "Three cheers for Bjarke! Three cheers for Olaf!"

"Olebjørn," the two-headed troll corrected. "Yer new captain's name be Olebjørn. We gained a second head for bigger threats."

"And bigger thoughts and bigger plans!" Phoebe said in return. "We'll teach those giants for springing a kraken on us!"

"Yeah!" shouted the crowd.

Olebjørn didn't correct them, steering the group instead around the room.

"This be the captain's table," said Bjarke, lumbering over and heaving their body into a smooth deep chair.

"I don't understand," Zaria said, conjuring a fleece blanket and settling into the icy seat beside them.

"I do," said Christoffer. At her questioning look he explained, "This is one of the rooms that Olaf – er, Olebjørn –"

"We be Olaf at the time. It be okay to be calling us Olaf then," said Olaf's head.

"This whole thing is a bit of a trip," said Filip, perching on the edge of Zaria's chair and sharing her blanket. "You've got two heads!"

"We do," Olebjørn agreed. "While we share heads our powers be joined and regenerate faster."

"What about your domains?" asked Aleks. "Bjarke's was the Norwegian Sea and Olaf's the Glomma, but we are in Efjorden."

"Domains not being shared," said Bjarke. "Our *Ursula* be gone and so be that domain."

"Aye," said Olaf. "The river-troll of the Efjorden is granting temporary amnesty. The story of our fight with the kraken be enough payment."

"Stories like that one don't come around every day," said Henrik, sitting down, Skorri swaying in the antlers above him.

"They do not."

"It was a good trade," he complimented. "There is much wisdom in the sharing and the hearing."

Zaria stared at the crew across the room before turning to them again. "Did you not have a bubble home in the sea? Did you truly lose your home when you lost *Ursula*?"

"We did," said Olaf. "Be not sad for us, Princess."

"Is there a dominant head?" asked Christoffer his gaze bouncing between them.

"Yes," said Olebjørn. "The first head is dominant."

"Oh," said Christoffer, thinking hard on the problem. "So that's Olaf?"

"We be Olebjørn," reminded Olebjørn gruffly. "Olaf and Bjarke are the river-trolls we once were, not the river-troll we being now."

Christoffer apologized. "I'm sorry. I meant no offense. I still see you as two trolls and not a two-headed troll."

"It be taking some getting used to we understand."

"Olaf said it was temporary," Aleks said. "Back on the bridge I mean when he was talking with Bjarke."

"When will you change back?" asked Geirr.

Olebjørn scratched at the scar joining the two halves. They gestured vaguely and said, "When the job we must be doing, be finished."

Henrik steepled his fingers and gazed over them. "Which job is that?"

"Restoring the Glomma and gathering allies for Queen Helena. She be trusting us with a monumental task."

"You can say that again," Geirr said shaking his head. "What is going on with the giants? How are they so blinded by Oskar the Elevated?"

"When a good leader turns bad, there be much hope, in the old guard, for that leader to return to the good one he once be," said Bjarke.

The sage words had Olaf's head nodding. "Then there be the new guard, they know not what's been lost but only what they see."

"Your speech is different," noted Zaria with wide eyes. "Almost as if it combined like your powers did."

"We not be noticing," said Olebjørn. "This just being the way we talk."

Filip asked, "What happens when you change back? You've said Bjarke lost his domain."

Bjarke's head answered, "The second head is rewarded for services rendered. There will be a new domain or help reclaiming the old."

Olebjørn clapped their hands and changed the subject. "The galley crew informs that dinner be ready."

The air in the room warmed and a short gusty breeze blew by, ruffling clothes and lifting hair. When it faded, the elves and ellefolken who'd worked the galley on Bjarke's ship, appeared in the center of the room. Wielding heaping trays of seafood soup, they wended around the room, distributing bowls to all.

Christoffer leaned over and inhaled the aroma rising from his bowl. "Is that crab?" he asked, prodding the white meat floating on the surface. "Are we really eating crab right now?"

Olebjørn smiled toothily from both heads. "Kraken is a rare treat."

"No way," said Geirr. "That gross thing? It was graying and covered in slime."

"We not be using those parts," the river-troll said with a twinkle. "Too chewy."

Filip spooned a mouthful and brought it to his lips. He ate it cautiously and stared wide-eyed at Zaria and the others. "It's delicious."

"Of course, it be," Olebjørn laughed. "It's fresh. Spoils of war. Now eat up."

"How did you harvest it?" asked Geirr. "We were down there with it. We didn't see you."

"Some river-troll magic as the maelstrom collapsed," Olebjørn said lightly, using two hands, one from each side of their body to eat. Both heads sighed in bliss at the first mouthfuls. "Oh, how long a time it's been since we be eating kraken."

Zaria poked at hers for a minute and tried it, taking a small bite of the crab meat and the broth. "It's good, but I feel bad eating it. Scary though it was, we've made the species extinct. It was the only one seen in over a millennium."

"Don't feel bad, Princess," said Henrik. "It's a rare delicacy and the next kraken is already being formed as we sit here. Some oversized hermit crab is leaving its shell now to sneak into the old one's home to grow and grow in darkness and safety."

"I thought the kraken didn't have a shell?" Christoffer said, eating his soup. "The one we fought didn't have one."

Henrik shrugged, "I don't think anyone knows for certain. It might have a massive hole or cave or trench it uses to hide in and only leaves its protection to hunt on the surface. Or maybe it really sheds its shell and never returns to one."

"We think it grows indefinitely," Olebjørn said, slurping another pair of spoonfuls.

Zaria shuddered at the thought, but dutifully ate more of her soup. Aleks fed morsels of crabmeat to Airi and Henrik offered some bites from his bowl to Skorri, who greedily ate his fill before burping and settling back into his perch on the Stag Lord's antlers. Christoffer, determined not to leave Defender out, saved some in his bowl and fed it to him under the table. In thanks he received a happy woof and a lick to the hand.

Those who finished eating, came to bid the two-headed troll goodnight. The departing crew left in short bursts of air at the wave of Olebjørn's hands. Christoffer yawned a few times – not because he was tired, although he was, as the long trek by bicycle through the coastline sapped him of energy – but to alleviate the pressure from the ongoing departures.

"What's next?" asked Filip, putting his utensils down and wiping his mouth. "Where exactly are we heading?"

Aleks answered, "South toward Malmdor."

"Our destination be a bit more southerly than that," Olebjørn said. "Yer navigation skills be remarkable."

"Are you taking us to Álfheim?" asked Zaria. "What about making alliances with the giants in the north?"

"We be dropping ye off there, yes. As for us, first we be scouting the Gjöll and Glomma," Olebjørn said, two sets of eyes narrowing in anger.

"Aye, there be something Oskar the Elevated said to his giants that be making us suspicious," said Olaf's head, stroking his chin.

"What do you expect to find?" breathed Zaria, worry clouding her eyes.

"You fear it's a dragon's army," Henrik said, his countenance darkening.

"Aye," said Bjarke's head. "We be sending our crew to scout the region. We be knowing more when ye return."

"Rest now," Olebjørn commanded. "There be more to do on the morrow."

Olebjørn provided them with quarters to share. The furnishings were sparse as Christoffer was accustomed to seeing. Zaria went about creating more beds for them to sleep on, cramming the small bubble space with mattresses, pillows, throws, and blankets.

"Where's the bathroom in this place?" asked Geirr.

Christoffer gestured to a small partition in the room. "It's on the other side of that."

Geirr made his way there and poked his head around the corner. "No way," he said, turning to give them a disgusted look. "It's a bucket."

"We're in a bubble? Were you expecting a full-size commode?" asked Christoffer. "Be glad there's a bucket."

"Do I even want to know?" asked Aleks.

"No," said Christoffer and Henrik at once.

"Zaria?" Geirr begged. "Can you give us something better than a bucket?"

She giggled and made her way over. Concentrating for a moment she managed to provide a toilet seat.

"Where's the rest of it?" Geirr asked, aghast.

"She's working on it," said Filip. He turned his green gaze on her. "You are working on it, aren't you Zar-Zar?"

Christoffer chuckled and left them to it, following Henrik back around the partition to the beds. He claimed one in the middle so he could be at the center of all talks. Defender clambered over to him and tucked in close. Laying a hand on his head, he gave him a few scratches.

Skorri landed nearby and nibbled on a few feathers. "Tell me more about this brownie," he demanded, but the demand was laced with apprehension.

Tilting his head back, Christoffer looked at the raven and shrugged. "I don't know too much about him."

"What do you know?" Skorri asked, knocking loudly in equal parts impatience and irritation.

"Master Brown guards a key strategic location between the realms of Trolgar and Álfheim. He very much wants a talking white raven. So much so, he once had five of them all at one time. None of them bonded with him though, and he wanted more."

"He must be deficient in some way if the other ravens didn't bond with him. And this is the creature you want me to call master?" He scoffed.

"Master Brown is well respected among his peers," said Henrik, having overheard. He settled into one of the beds nearby, groaning as his muscles relaxed.

"Other blue creatures like him, so what?" Skorri huffed, nibbling on a talon.

"In their culture, you don't earn a mastery unless it's deserved," Henrik explained. "He's also got a good rapport with trolls and elves, no easy feat. The two races are diametrically opposite each other."

"Yeah," Christoffer agreed. "Trolls prize strength and size, the bigger the better. How could they respect Master Brown, whose stature is so small, unless he had a true gift at diplomacy and the ability to back up his words and actions?"

Aleks sunk into bed on the other side of him. "Right, and the elves are not about brute strength, but cunning and culture. They love knowledge, science, and illusions. Master Brown has to be on equal footing with them, as well."

"Strength and skill," Airi concluded, landing beside the fey king's pillow.

Skorri knocked low in his throat, thinking many thoughts. "Then why isn't he your master, then? Were you not one of his pets?"

Airi clucked. "He is not as good as my Aleks."

"I should be Aleks' white raven," said Skorri.

Airi launched herself at Skorri before Aleks could stop her. She screamed, clawing and biting the other raven. The ruckus could wake the dead and startled Christoffer half out of his skin. Feathers went flying and both birds were cursing each other. The commotion had Defender barking and braying as he tried to get involved. Filip collared him, keeping him from the fray.

Aleks caught Airi, and was trying to pry her off the other raven but to no avail. She was fierce in her rebuttal, giving Skorri no room to flee or recover. Afraid blood would start flying, Christoffer inserted himself into the fight and managed to snatch Skorri from harm's away. For his efforts, he received a vicious peck that drew the blood he'd been trying to prevent.

"Ow," he shouted, cussing under his breath and nursing the wound. "Damn birds. This is why a dog is better."

"Dogs bite too, you dunderhead," screeched Skorri mutinously, trying to free himself from Christoffer's clutches. "LET ME GO!"

Airi flapped hard, trying to pull away from Aleks, shrieking, "You're dunderhead. You're dunderhead."

"Enough," said Aleks, stopping her with a hand around her beak. She pecked him hard and he winced, but he didn't let go until she calmed.

"Your raven is rabid," sniffed Skorri.

"Don't start," warned Aleks. "You started this. Airi is my white raven. I am not looking for another."

"I didn't really want to be your white raven anyway," Skorri retorted. Christoffer released him and he flew-hopped to the opposite side of the room where Zaria and Filip were trying to settle.

"You will like Master Brown," Zaria whispered to the raven. "You are more alike than you think."

"We shall wait and see," Skorri said dubiously, tucking his head under his wing. "I'm not holding my breath."

"That's okay," she said. "You just promised to meet him."

"That's right. Only promised to meet the brownie."

"You know you made him proud," she said softly. The raven peeked at her from behind his wing. She smiled and brushed the soft downy feathers on his head. He closed his steel-blue eyes in pleasure, making a soft chuffing sound. "It's true. You're giving yourself a chance to find new happiness and purpose. That's a huge step. He would be pleased at your efforts."

Christoffer thought she might be right. Giants, despite the recent skirmishes with the Seiland clan, were genuinely delighted and contented in the goodness that happened to others. Skorri's old master, now transformed back into a mountain, would want more for his raven than mourning. This would be a good chance for Skorri to have a full and fulfilling life again. He simply had to give it a chance.

"Go to sleep," she coaxed, and the raven and the others shifted, sighing as they settled into beds for the night.

Christoffer laid back, one hand behind his head and the other lightly shifting through Defender's fur to stare at the rippling shapes and shadows above. He thought about second chances, second nature, second winds, and secondary heads. With his thoughts drifting there wasn't any rhyme or reason to the thoughts that came to him and slipped away like silver fish.

As sleep washed over him a pair of red lips hovered at the edges of his consciousness. He snorted and tried to bat them away, more interested in dreaming about having a second talking head on his shoulders. The lips persisted, but he paid them no mind until they suddenly morphed onto the second head and his other half tried to kiss him.

That woke him up with a heart-pounding start. Laughing weakly under his breath as the dream faded, he settled back down, comforting a questioning Defender who had woken up with him. Falling back asleep he said, "Someone please tell me I'm not that narcissistic."

"You are," Skorri rejoined.

"Heh, burn," Christoffer said, keeping his eyes closed. "You know, because it's coming from you?"

The white raven scoffed and hid behind his wing again. Defender nestled under his arm, resting his nose near Christoffer's armpit. Soon all three fell back asleep and the dream and the conversation were forgotten.

Chapter Six: The Gulley

The next day after Zaria had magically vanished all their beds and linens, Olebjørn dropped the whole group off near Gloomwood, then continued south to their river, the Glomma. Christoffer and the others bid them *adieu* thanking them for the escort to Álfheim. Zaria watched them return to their home through the whirlpool and the waters close over their heads. She shared an anxious glance with Filip and Aleks.

"They'll be fine," Christoffer said. "If you'd seen the dining room as it was before, you would understand. It was melted and mangled – wholly unrecognizable as a dining room. Last night, not only was it not melted, but it had designs carved on all the surfaces."

"Trust them to know what needs doing," Filip said, giving her hand a squeeze.

She sighed. "It's hard not to worry. The dangers surrounding this dragon are mounting. I can't even imagine what will happen next."

Henrik handed Zaria her bag, saying, "It's better not to anticipate troubles. We need only focus ourselves on the next step."

"And the next one after that," Filip agreed. "Eventually they get us where we need to be."

"Right," said Christoffer, pumping a fist. "Kicking dragon butt. If it's anything like kicking kraken butt, it'll be tasty."

Henrik looked a little nauseated. "I don't intend to ingest dragon."

"It might taste like chicken," he said, waggling his eyebrows.

The Stag Lord shook his head. "Hard pass. Until Zaria, there were no dead ones to eat. I don't have any desire to try dragon now that there are."

"Well, yeah..." agreed Christoffer. "That's because Koll and Fritjof have been dead for several years. I wouldn't recommend eating them either."

"Your mind goes in really strange directions," Aleks commented, shouldering his bag. "How about we go where mine leads instead?"

"My directions are more fun," Christoffer said.

"Mine, however, are practical," Aleks teased. "So, you know, we actually get where we want to go."

With that, the group commenced the journey, traveling southeast into the woods. The ravens flew in tandem overhead, wheeling through the sky, high in the thermals. Defender trotted at his heels and Christoffer kept his eyes peeled for the first sign of Gloomwood and the home of the elves.

Oak, pine, and spruce slowly gave way to a forest of aspen, alder, and birch. Henrik and Aleks navigated together now, as the Stag Lord helped them to skirt some trickier places to climb and traverse. They crossed a small stream, too small to be of desire to a river-troll and not robust enough to be filled with wild magic, which disappointed Christoffer.

At first, he thought it to be the Gjöll, the wild river wound into Gloomwood Forest. Part of it did, anyway. The majority of the river flowed into the Under Realm, a magical realm crafted by master fey void designers.

The river was another guard against the dragons and its wild magic formed vicious, steel-flashing knives ready to cut intruders and escapees into ribbons, draining them of their magic. The little stream lacked the knives so in the end, it couldn't be the Gjöll.

Names were a funny thing. Calling this place Gloomwood Forest didn't make much sense to Christoffer. It wasn't as if the forest was gloomier now than it had been a moment ago. Though there wasn't a line to demarcate the difference between the woods from before and the woods they were now in, Henrik assured them they were in the heart of Álfheim. The heart (and hart) of Gloomwood Forest, so integral to their past adventures, lay in the Glade of the Golden Kings, much further east than they were going.

"Our destination is just beyond this next hill," said Henrik, pointing ahead.

"We don't want to go that way," Aleks said suddenly, stopping Geirr from stepping forward.

"What? Why not?" he asked. "We're so close to Edevart's and Frida's place, not to mention her homecooked meals."

"Don't talk about food," Filip moaned. "I'm so hungry."

Christoffer rubbed his belly, pouting. "It's because Zaria's determined to starve us."

She quirked an eyebrow at them and crossed her arms. "Really? See if I make the lot of you provisions again."

Christoffer grabbed her wrist. "You wouldn't really starve us, would you?" He batted his lashes and pouted more, causing her to laugh and shove him away.

"Why don't we want to travel this way?" asked Henrik.

Airi wheeled down from the sky and landed in a tree. "Banshees, ahead," she warned.

"How did you know that?" Zaria asked Aleks.

He shrugged, running a hand through his hair. "Just a feeling. My internal map wants to route us a different way."

Henrik glared in the direction of the banshees. "Can you tell how many?"

Aleks shook his head. "No, but I know danger awaits us if we go that way."

Considering banshees could freeze you into place and turn you to stone with just the sound of their voices, Christoffer agreed that way was dangerous; but with a sharp knife and some Grade A earplugs you could safely get by them by shorning their hair. He wondered how closely related they were to hulders who could ensnare you with their voices and were also readily defended against with earplugs. Neat how that worked and a stroke of luck for them.

As a side note, fortunately – for him – the banshees looked like dead lifeless things compared to the spirited lively hulders. No temptations there to kiss any of them.

"It's out of the way, but we could travel that way. There's a glen and a –"

"No," Aleks said, shaking his head again. "We don't want to go that way either."

Henrik raised an eyebrow in surprise. "More banshees?"

"No," said Skorri alighting on the branch next to Airi. "It's an ogre. He's turning the trunk of a tree into a new club to smash his prey with right now and scratching his crotch with the leafy bits."

"And in that direction," Aleks said softly, keeping his voice low, "there's a hag and her pack of wolverines."

"That's awfully specific," Geirr commented. "Your navigation skills are growing."

"Yes," he said. "Or crystalizing; things are clearer than they used to be in many ways."

Christoffer caught the fey king's play of words and gave him a thumbs up. At Aleks' bemused look, he said, "Because the fairy kingdom builds with crystals."

"I wish I could've said pun intended," Aleks said with a shrug. "I didn't even catch that, but I'll stick to my word choice. My magic is crystalizing. I sense it."

"We shall trust that and go this way, across the gulley," the Stag Lord said, pausing and waiting for Aleks to contradict him.

"That way feels safe," the fey king said.

"Then that way it is," said Christoffer cheerfully, and Defender woofed happily.

Through the trees, away from banshees and ogres, the group walked. The gulley's embankment cut steeply down to a rocky floor before climbing upward at nearly the same angle it had gone down. Falling down would stupendously suck, but it wouldn't be deadly.

Taking rope from his bag, Geirr anchored it around a nearby tree and threw it over the ledge. Aleks descended first to spot him from below. After Geirr went, Zaria and Filip followed. With Henrik's help, he lowered Defender in a sling-like carrier to the ground below. Christoffer let the Stag Lord go next and then removed the rope from the tree and tossed it down to others who were waiting.

"What are you doing?" asked Zaria, alarmed as Christoffer shifted his body and weight to begin the descent.

He called over his shoulder, "Climbing."

"I know that, but why aren't you using the rope?"

"Because unlike in the Lost Well, this rope won't disappear on its own," he said, carefully wedging his feet into crags and working his way down.

"With banshees, hags, and an ogre about, it's not a bad idea to take it with us," said Geirr.

"Hey," he complained. "I'm known to have good ideas."

"On occasion, mate," Filip teased. "Only on a rare occasion."

Zaria crossed her arms, looking annoyed. "Sorceress, remember? I could vanish the rope."

"True," agreed Christoffer hopping down the rest of the way and landing with a thump. "But we're going to need it to climb out the other side."

"How are we going to anchor it?" asked Henrik.

"I can lead," Christoffer offered, taking the rope and coiling it around his arm. "I'm pretty good at free form."

"You're pretty good at breaking your neck," Zaria retorted. "My magic can't fix that!"

"You can just magic me another head," he said. At her horrified look, he added, "Don't fret, Zaria, I got this."

"Just what are you trying to prove?" she demanded.

Widening his eyes innocently, he said, "What do you think I am trying to prove?"

"That you contribute," she said hotly. "And you do, you know. We need you. What we don't need is you falling off a cliff trying to be a superhero."

"It's not that far a fall," Christoffer said, alarm creeping into his voice at her shimmering gaze.

"Not that far," she huffed, angry and worried.

She grabbed his arm. He felt the hairs rise in warning, and with a snap, they were above on the other side of the gulley. He waved meekly down to the others. "Okay, okay, you win. Don't go getting your tiara in a twist," he said, awkwardly patting her arm which wound tight about his chest.

"Your safety is important. You're being far too reckless. You might say you're nimble like a goat, but you should take precautions."

"Hey mate, Zar-Zar," Filip shouted, looking a little hesitant, while Geirr and Aleks nudged him forward. "Are we climbing or being teleported?"

"Climbing the rope," said Christoffer, side-eyeing Zaria to see if she had any objections.

While he anchored his end of the rope, she sent the other end down to their friends. Filip scrambled up first and wrapped Zaria in a tentative hug. She clung to him, discretely hiding tears. Watching her gather her emotions, Christoffer felt guilty. He hadn't realized just how much he'd scared her with his cavalier attitude. Climbing was really something he didn't think much about, as he felt confident in his abilities, much like Aleks did in his navigation.

"Zaria, it's okay," he told her, reaching out to lay a comforting hand on her shoulder. "I promise. I don't have a death wish."

"Good," she sniffled. "I don't know why I got so scared. It was almost irrational."

"Almost?" he teased.

She scowled at him. "But you, you just keep risking yourself. I couldn't – None of us could stand losing you. What would Moon and Star do without you? You have to be sensible. I nearly lost you all during the maelstrom. What if my magic had been just a little bit slower or not as powerful? You would have plummeted to your deaths."

The thought of his sisters sobered him and he nodded. He'd not noticed how stressed she'd been about their near misses. He might tease her otherwise, but to him she was infallible with her powers, if a little shy to use them. He trusted she'd keep them all safe.

Christoffer returned her hug when she wrapped him in one, squeezing tight. When she let him go, she vigorously scrubbed her eyes, hiding tears. Filip pressed a kiss to her temple and her answering smile only wavered slightly along the edges.

When everyone, including Defender, was up out of the gulley, Zaria had composed herself. They all made promises to her to be cautious and not to run headfirst into dangers unknown. Christoffer was grateful that her weak smile grew more solid at their assurances.

Geirr stowed the rope back in his bag and they continued onward through the morning. The gulley and indirect path slowed their quest for Álfheim. When they reached the elf's city, it was almost noon. Sweaty, tired, and still recovering a bit from Zaria's unexpected emotional onslaught, the group descended on Queen Silje's realm ready to eat, sleep, and recover.

Being back in Álfheim evoked everything Christoffer remembered. Frosted glass spires and stairs wound up and around trees, creating awe-inspiring spectacles with soaring heights and delicate lacy visages. Homes shimmered as if dusted by confectioner's sugar, reaching high in the canopies. Bridges linked them all in one giant tree house formation. The whole glade appeared to be set on fire with the fall leaves' vibrant red, orange, and yellow hues reflecting from every surface.

News of their arrival swept the glade and elves and ellefolken appeared out of the woodwork like ants. Many greeted Henrik warmly, inquiring after his health and adventures. Female ellefolken babes were presented to be blessed by kisses to their foreheads, which Henrik did with an obliging smile, patting heads and chucking chins, while discussing trivialities with their parents. Some of the bolder mothers and their older daughters passed on sweets, meats, and pelts to him, much like those in Elleken had when he'd departed. He graciously took all that he could, and rejected kindly that which he could not hold.

Disappointed faces reluctantly held onto their offerings and stepped back as he strode through their midst toward the center of the city. Christoffer thought Henrik did well in these encounters. Gracious and friendly, by accepting as many as he could, Henrik favored none. Of course, he could do the opposite and take nothing from any of them. Then he'd be considered rude and aloof, but still princely and desirable, like so many of the male leads in Christoffer's mother's favorite dramas. At least Henrik's approach didn't necessarily hurt tender feelings and was an act of kindness.

"Welcome stranger," a cordial tenor called from the crowd, which separated to reveal a familiar face.

"Edevart," Henrik greeted warmly to the pale blond elf. "I see you're still growing out your beard. It's starting to fill in to match your mustache."

Edevart fingered it circumspectly. "It's taking some getting used to, but the little one loves it."

"And the wife?" teased Henrik, mirth crinkling the edges of his eyes.

"She is getting used to it, too," he laughed. "Come, follow me. Frida and my little Lisebet are waiting for us back at the house."

"How old is she?" asked Christoffer, feeling suddenly and unexpectedly homesick for his twin sisters.

Beaming, Edevart gestured with long tapered fingers. "She's just had her eighth lunar-versary."

"Lunar-versary?" Christoffer asked, confused. "Do you mean she's eight months old?"

The proud father nodded. "You'll love her. She's the happiest baby."

"I can't wait to hold her," said Zaria eagerly. "I bet she's just the most precious thing ever."

"That she is, Princess," he said, leading them up into the trees and along the walkways.

Frida cried out in joy at their arrival, shifting baby Lisebet to her other hip. The little elf baby was chubby, with little fat rolls all over and pale, nearly colorless, wispy blonde hair that fluttered about like a baby duck's downy feathers. She had a ruddy complexion and the widest blue eyes that stared about watchfully at them as they approached. Her mother handed her over to Zaria's outstretched arms happily and let the two get acquainted while turning to her other guests and ushering them all inside.

The ravens roosted in nearby branches while Christoffer left Defender outside to guard the door, not trusting him inside where they had many breakable things. It wasn't exactly baby friendly, and because Lisebet didn't appear to get much time out of people's arms, it probably didn't matter.

Frida whipped up a meaty snack for all their animal companions to enjoy and took it outside. Defender stood at attention in an instant; the birds above were more speculative but soon swooped down. The border collie munched on his bone, while the ravens greedily gulped down the pink flesh.

One of the ravens made a knocking sound, Christoffer didn't know who, while the other one cried out loudly causing everyone to jump. Sudden unhappy barking jarred already frayed nerves. He and the others ran outside to see what the commotion was. Not spying them in the trees, he followed the direction of Defender's frowning stare. On the ground, far below, the ravens gleefully ripped flesh in turns from his dog's bone.

"That's rude," he shouted down to them. "You had your meal."

Their knocking sounded like laughter and Christoffer frowned at Aleks. He held up his hands in surrender. "Airi has a mind of her own."

"You can afford to teach her manners," he said.

Frida tsked and ushered Defender into her home, waving to staring neighbors from nearby trees. "Those white ravens may have tricked you, poor thing, but don't despair I have more morsels for you to eat. Better ones even than those you lost."

She pitched her voice to carry down to the ravens below, who suddenly appeared upset and intrigued. Abandoning their prize, they flew up to the rail and peered inside with beady eyes. Christoffer shut the door in their face with a sharp snap, daring Skorri, but especially Airi to complain.

"Rude," she called back to him, making him laugh.

"Serves you right," he said through the door.

Inside, Defender was given a ladleful of the meal that had been stewing on the hearth. Contented, he wolfed it down, sparing only the slightest glance at the closed front door.

"Those nasty ravens can't steal your food," Christoffer assured him.

"Hey," complained Aleks. "Just who are you calling nasty?"

He stuck out his tongue. "Your white raven. She starts hanging out with this Skorri scamp and picks up all these bad habits. And tell me, is she sorry at all? No!"

"She's not sorry," Zaria said, blowing Lisebet raspberry kisses on her belly, making the baby laugh. "She's Airi."

"Ha!" Christoffer laughed.

"Ravens have been known to work together to steal food," Henrik cut in before Aleks could retort. "It's not Aleks' fault your dog got tricked."

Christoffer grinned. "Oh, I know, but I can't help giving him a hard time. Besides, Defender seems happy enough now. Still, man, you want to keep an eye on that suitor of hers. He's trouble."

Aleks spluttered. "Suitor? What?"

"He's kidding," soothed Filip. He looked up. "You are kidding, right?"

"Relax," said Geirr, seeing his best friend's sudden apoplectic look. "Airi's not going to fall for a raven, no matter how smart he is, once he's called her some names. She's too prideful for that."

"We have more important matters to discuss than the mating behaviors of ravens," Aleks said, face red. "Like dragons."

"Dragons?" Frida asked in alarm.

Aleks nodded. "And krakens."

"Krakens?" Edevart asked, eyebrows rising toward the ceiling in surprise.

He nodded again. "And increased activity in the woods…"

"I'm almost afraid to ask," Frida said, plucking Lisebet from Zaria's arms and holding her close. "What sort of adventure are you all on now?"

"Didn't you hear about the goblins?" Filip asked, looking surprised. "It all started with them."

Chapter Seven: Odd Couple

At the end of their tale, Edevart let out a gusty sigh and finger-combed his mustache. His gaze was heavy and speculative as he took them in, contemplating the next move. With a small shake of his head, he said, "It's always dragons with you lot. Why is that?"

Christoffer laughed, amused. "When isn't it about dragons with us?"

Frida busied herself in the kitchen and fretted. "I feared something like this would happen. Didn't I tell you when we spoke of starting our family?"

"You did," her husband agreed. He encircled her and the baby in his arms and she stilled in the strength of his embrace. Pressing a soft kiss to Lisebet's hair, he continued, "We can't live our lives in fear of the next dragon attack. Besides, it was calm then, and if we had waited, we wouldn't have Lisebet now. I know you wouldn't do anything differently. I wouldn't either."

"Why are the dragons stirring so much?" she asked, breaking free, clanging around, and putting away dishes. "I remember when the incidents of dragon movement and machinations were ages apart."

"Centuries even," agreed Henrik solemnly. He canted his head to the side and looked at the new parents. "Still, Edevart is right. You wouldn't trade Lisebet for more safety and peaceful times."

She sighed in frustration and then pressed a tender kiss to the baby in her arms. "We can't lose her. I couldn't bear it. We need to make preparations to safeguard her and our home from both goblins and dragons."

"There're other creatures edging closer to your city," said Aleks. "We circumnavigated around an ogre and some banshees."

Edevart frowned. "We knew about those. We tend to let the other creatures be, so long as they don't provoke us. With humans gradually encroaching on more and more territory, it's important to find ways to live together."

"I don't like it," said Frida, wiping down the counter.

"I don't like it either," her husband said. "What worries me most isn't the goblins or dragons, but why Queen Silje hasn't made the news public. Our patrols should have been and should now be made aware of the dangers. Those watching the city's entrances should know to be on guard."

Frida nodded, throwing her towel into the sink. "I'm so grateful you operate the lift. If you're to be kept in the dark then that is the safest place to guard."

"When we last spoke, she indicated she would investigate what happened at the Gjallarbrú," said Henrik. "Perhaps it is still being investigated?"

"Right," said Zaria. "It hasn't been that many days."

Geirr shook his head. "I disagree. It's been over a week; in fact, it's nearly been two."

Edevart slapped the table releasing pent-up frustration. "She's had more than enough time to prepare a preliminary report and get it out to all of us."

"What could she mean by it?" asked Aleks.

"I intend to find out, but not before I see you all on your way," he said. "Because of how information is being withheld or shared, it's best to get you out of Álfheim. You shouldn't be detained, not even for the queen's investigation."

"There must be a perfectly reasonable explanation," Zaria hedged, hating to see conflict amongst the elves.

"If there is, I will get it," Edevart said firmly. "You're on important business. You need not trouble yourselves. I have a lot at stake. Trust me when I say I'll get to the bottom of this."

"We do trust you," said Zaria, reaching out her hands to clasp both of theirs. She looked at father and mother alike. "Both of you."

Frida's eyes misted. "You are a dear girl, Princess Zaria."

"When this is over," Zaria said. "I want to come back and visit with you properly. There hasn't been nearly enough time to get to know Lisebet."

"Trolgar?" Edevart asked, standing up and pushing in his chair.

"Not quite," said Geirr. "We're going to see Master Brown."

"Oh ho," said Edevart in surprise. "He doesn't get many visitors strictly seeking him out."

"I don't imagine he does," said Christoffer, eyes twinkling.

"Is that why you have two white ravens?" Edevart asked, leading them out of his house and back down to the base of the trees.

Filip nodded. "He's agreed to meet with the brownie— "

Christoffer interrupted, "Well, only after we beat him in a series of challenges and discovered the name of the last guy he served."

"I knew there must have been more to your story. When you return, tell me that tale. I think I need a little levity after all this heavy news you lot have dropped in my lap."

The elf guided them to a spot off-center from the circle of trees and buildings they'd just left. The grass here looked more vibrant than the grass a few feet away. On a nearby tree, Edevart pressed two hands against the trunk. It clicked opened to reveal a hollow with a dial, a horn, and a lever.

Picking up the horn, which acted like an old-fashioned kid's phone, Edevart called out. "Hello, Master Brown? You have visitors."

"Visitors?" came a high-pitched nasally voice. "I am not expecting visitors. Don't be fooled. They're probably solicitors. Send them away."

"They're not solicitors," Edevart said, his eyes crinkling. "Trust me, you want to see them."

"No, no," said Master Brown. "I'm too busy, too busy. If they truly wish to see me, they can come back tomorrow."

Edevart laughed. "Good sir, you must be truly busy indeed to turn away a white raven."

A loud shriek echoed in the clearing, causing Edevart and the others to flinch. He ran a finger in his ear to clear it out and cautiously brought the horn closer. "Master Brown?"

A suspicious voice answered, "Did you say a white raven? Did I hear you right? This better not be some cruel joke, Edevart, because I'm telling you, if it be a solicitor, I will make you regret ever being born."

"It's not a joke," he said, solemnly, putting his hand against his heart. "You remember Princess Zaria and her good friends? The Stag Lord and King Aleks are also here."

"How come we're never mentioned?" Christoffer griped, crossing his arms.

"And also their courageous friends: Christoffer, Geirr, and Filip," Edevart amended with a wink to him, acknowledging the error.

"Is it one white raven with them?" Master Brown questioned. "I heard King Aleks took one of my ravens for his own."

"Two ravens," said Edevart.

"They both talk?" Master Brown pressed.

Edevart chuckled. "I have heard both talking, yes. Come now, open your side of the lift so they can come down to you. You offend them any more by continuing to doubt them and they may take the white raven elsewhere."

"Don't let them leave!" barked the anxious brownie.

There was a loud click and Edevart gave them a thumbs up before hanging up. He pulled the lever and the ground began to rumble and crack apart. Small stones skittered and danced at Christoffer's feet. The hole widened and the vibrant grassy circle retracted, sliding under the ground.

Tempted to look over the edge, Filip stepped closer.

"Watch your step," the elf warned, throwing an arm out to stop him. "There're no rails on this side. I don't want you to fall."

"Good call," he said, moving back. "Zar-Zar might be able to save me if I fell, but let's not risk it."

"I appreciate that," she said, clutching his hand and holding it tight. "I prefer my boyfriends to be alive."

The opening suddenly spat water at them and Christoffer threw his hands in front of him. Half-turned away, he shouted, "Is this elevator part camel or something?"

"The platform has arrived," said Edevart laughingly. "Give me a moment."

Indeed, the hole in the ground was filled with a round metallic platform. Held aloft by water pressure from below, the elevator hovered in place next to them. Christoffer watched Edevart turn some dials and flip some switches.

A small bridge of glass extended to the center of the opening, connecting where they stood to the floating island. Airi gazed on in interest from Aleks' shoulder and Skorri from Henrik's antlers. Defender sat next to him and panted warmly against his leg.

"You can climb on now," their elven companion said, and one by one they filed across the short bridge to the hovering platform.

"Hold onto the railing," Henrik advised, gripping the rail in front of them.

Christoffer and the others copied him and when they were settled to Edevart's satisfaction he bid them goodbye. A few more twists and turns on the dials, another pull on the lever, and the floor began to drift downward.

Christoffer could feel the solid surface under his feet, but the steady decrease in water pressure made him feel like he was falling. Controlled falling, but falling nonetheless. A glance toward Geirr showed his friend gripping the railing so tightly his knuckles started to turn white.

When their heads cleared the opening, Edevart waved. They waved back and the ceiling began to grumble and creak as it closed, blocking out all available natural light. Zaria lifted a hand off the rail and a bright flame of light spread from her fingertips. The walls of the cave were washed in purple and the platform lowered faster going down and down some more.

Soon, they were level with the realm managed by Master Brown. The roar of running water echoed in Christoffer's ears, drowning out all other sounds. Fireflies danced around his head, landing briefly in his hair and on his skin before alighting again. The creaky wooden waterwheel rumbled steadily as the buckets feeding it tottered and trembled. They filed lazily to the leaky wooden aqueduct that routed water from a naturally occurring waterfall against the cavern wall and back again to the wheel. The buckets lost more water than they retained, dumping it back into the dark, small pool below.

At the center of the cave, by his version of the control box, stood Master Brown on a small stool. He practically vibrated in excitement and nervous energy. Watching their progress, the old brownie made adjustments on his dials, turning knobs and flipping switches. His bare blue feet tapped nervously as he waited for their arrival.

When his excitement became too much and he couldn't take it anymore, Master Brown pulled a lever and the platform collapsed the final few feet, landing on the floor with a bang and rattling into place. Geirr jumped and Christoffer felt his heart racing in his chest as he got his bearings. The rail whooshed and snapped toward the ground, freeing them to escape the water elevator.

Before even one of them could exit the platform, Master Brown was beside them, staring with wide, dark predatory eyes at Skorri, perched in Henrik's antlers. His entire body vibrated with barely contained emotion. Rubbing his hands nervously he gave a short bow and squeaked, "Welcome to my home."

"Thank you," Zaria said graciously, and his head snapped up.

He glared. "I wasn't talking to you."

Nonplussed, she stared agape at his rudeness. Henrik laid a calming hand on her shoulder and moved away. "Shall we gather inside your home and make formal introductions?" he asked.

The brownie tracked his movement, his eyes never leaving Skorri. The white raven watched him, too, strangely silent as they sized each other up.

"Would you like to see my home?" Master Brown spoke without turning his gaze. Defender woofed and the brownie's attention slanted sideways. "Who brought the dog?" he asked with contempt.

Christoffer waved. "I did."

"The dog stays outside."

"You heard about Olaf's living room, didn't you?" Christoffer asked, shaking his head at the border collie. "What did I tell you? All it takes is one gjallarhorn call and your manners are known all over the country. Nobody trusts you."

Defender woofed and licked his hand. He petted the top of his head and scratched behind his ears. "Defender, beg."

Obediently, the border collie sat on his haunches and whined softly, his eyes widening and watering. Hugging him close, Christoffer looked up at the brownie. "How can you say no to this face?"

"Easily," said Master Brown dryly. "No."

"Aw," pouted Christoffer. "How come?"

"He's too big and ill-mannered for my place," the brownie said, crossing his arms. "I think you mentioned something happening at Olaf's place? That river-troll's realm is big enough for four or five Masters. If your mutt didn't do well there, he's not invited to my home."

"No problem," said Aleks, giving Christoffer a look. "We'll leave the dog outside."

"Outside," Airi agreed, ruffling her feathers as she perched on Aleks' shoulder, looking a bit smug.

Master Brown's beady black eyes focused on Airi with a mix of greed and disgust. "I remember you," he told her.

The raven nibbled on a talon. "I remember you."

"Talking now, I see," he said contemplatively. "You were silent before him."

She tittered and pecked on his earlobe affectionately. "My Aleks is handsome."

At this absurd pronouncement, the brownie harrumphed and so did Skorri. They eyed each other hesitantly. A moment passed and Master Brown cracked a tentative smile. "I'll repeat my offer, Master Raven. Do you wish to see my home?"

Skorri dipped his head, a regal air about his brow. With the raven perched above, it was difficult to get an accurate picture, but he looked nearly as big as the brownie. Master Brown just about reached their waists, and Christoffer figured the bird was about two feet tall like Airi and Defender.

"Follow me," he said, turning back toward his home, hidden inside the cave's walls.

With a firm push, Master Brown wedged open the metallic door. A soft lilting melody, nearly drowned out by the waterfall, drifted out from the home's exposed depths. The brownie stepped aside to let them through. Christoffer left Defender in place to *down* and *stay*. He did without complaint.

Henrik folded up his golden-antlered cloak and left it next to the entrance outside. Defender sniffed at it curiously from where he stayed and deciding it was nothing, closed his eyes. Skorri flew into the house, impatient to see what lay inside. Frankly, so was Christoffer. It was like seeing something taboo, or better yet, by exclusive special access. He'd never seen where any brownie lived, just where they'd worked.

The interior room was roughly carved from the stone walls of the cave. Rugs littered the floor, overlapping and crisscrossing each other. Warm candlelight flickered from a myriad of candlesticks, all at various heights, scattered across numerous surfaces. Soft music played on a record player powered by magic. A bookshelf was cut into the stone.

The spines of the books had faded lettering from much use, but, even so, some titles were legible: *For the Discerning Palette: How to Fricassee Anything; A Thousand Years of Documented Conflict between Trolgar and Álfheim; Bridges: The Brownie's Guide to Avoiding River-Trolls; Among Brownies and Trolls; You Earned Your Master, Now What?; The Ultimate Guide to Gatekeeping, Guarding, and Gardening;* and finally, *The Illusions of Elves*.

Pictures of brownies and landscapes dotted the walls, depicting an array of locations and times. Perhaps it was his family's history, or maybe things he found enjoyable, a way to bring the outdoors in, since he had no windows. A rounded hallway, cluttered with canvases led off to the left with a hint of a staircase.

The living room directly behind the metal door featured low ceilings despite the promise of the staircase just out of sight. All the boys had to duck or crouch a little, unable to stand fully upright. Only Zaria could stand up straight. Christoffer weaved around a wagon wheel chandelier with a mess of melting candles and slung himself into one of the brownie's overstuffed couches.

"Be careful," Master Brown admonished. "Not all my furniture can withstand a human male's aggressions."

"Oh sorry," said Christoffer, grinning winningly.

"Skorri," huffed the male white raven, clipping the back of his head as it flew over him.

Delighted, Christoffer clapped his hands. "You made a joke!"

"I'll bring down a pot of coffee and tea," Master Brown offered, eyeing the interaction with wariness. "Would you care for anything? I can bring some tasty bugs down."

"I could eat," Airi replied.

Skorri tutted and rolled his eyes. "He was talking to me, you dimwitted featherhead."

"I'll be right back," said Master Brown. "Please make yourself comfortable."

It was clear he meant the white ravens, but Filip and Geirr took the opportunity to fold themselves down into plump little chairs. Henrik wandered the room, admiring the pictures on the walls, touching one here or there and straightening it.

A window seat, cut into one wall and minus the actual window, called to Zaria. It overflowed with a motley set of pillows, books, scraps of paper, and a moth-eaten blanket. She'd begun to fold it and set it aside when Master Brown returned.

He frowned, noting the condition and snapped his fingers. The blanket disappeared and the books rearranged themselves into neat stacks on the floor. The paper tidied itself, settling on top of a barrel nearby. Even the dust disappeared, not foolish enough to stick around when a master brownie was showcasing his skills.

"I'm sorry you had to see that, I wasn't expecting company this evening," Master Brown said sheepishly, a purple flush creeping up the back of his neck.

"Your mastery is impressive," said Skorri, taking in the changes to the room. He clicked his beak. "One snap."

"Thank you," said Master Brown, his flush lingering under a renewed bloom.

Henrik made the formal introductions, providing the raven with details of Master Brown's background and then the sad history of Skorri's previous master. During the retellings, Airi and Skorri settled themselves on a small hammock and a coat rack occupying one corner.

Master Brown dropped a plate of morsels on the barrel sitting in front of them. Watching the ravens devour the proffered wriggling worms and buzzing insects made Christoffer glad not to be a bird. The disgusting creepy crawlers and their unfortunate crunchy companions did not appeal to him at all.

Not for nothing, the brownie presented each of them with a cup and a saucer. The fine china clinked delicately when Christoffer picked it up. He watched Master Brown study the ravens, a hint of pride appearing on his lips as the birds finished every last juicy morsel.

Skorri burped, covering his beak with one wing. "My compliments to the chef."

Master Brown grinned unguardedly. "I am glad you enjoyed them. It would be standard fare."

Skorri cleared his throat, knocking a little nervously. "Let's get down to business. I lost a bet with these children and promised to meet you. I didn't promise to stay."

Master Brown shared a glance with Henrik. "Stag Lord?"

"We could not in good conscience force him, a sentient being, to stay where he did not wish to stay."

"I see," he said. "If Skorri decides I do not suit him, what then?"

Henrik shrugged, "I suppose we'll have to find another way to complete our dealings and fulfill our promise to you."

The brownie nodded thoughtfully and settled himself near the white ravens. He asked, "What would make you stay with me?"

Skorri cawed, "Why do you seek a white raven?"

"If you agreed to be my white raven, I suppose you'd have a right to know. My daughter lives far away. She has two boys, and her husband died in the Battle of Koll's Bane. He lost a fight with a hag and was eaten by one of her wolverines."

"I know it well. We lost many good giants during Koll's Bane," Skorri said, cleaning his feathers.

Master Brown wrung his hands together. "Since the battle my daughter hasn't answered a single call on the horn. Not one. Nor have any others been able to find her. I've even tried human postal service. I am worried. If she's alive, I must find her. If she is not, I need to find her boys."

"That was three years ago," said Zaria, her eyebrows knitting together in alarm. "You haven't heard from your daughter or grandsons since? Why didn't they write to you?"

"The boys are too young to write," he explained. "I need to ensure their safety and welfare and hers as well. They should be near the Eastern Court of Jötunheim."

"In Finland, with Rubus the Golden?" Henrik asked.

The brownie hopped off his seat and went to one of the bookcases. He grabbed something small and square – a postcard – and handed it to the Stag Lord. "This is the last missive I've received."

Looking to the ravens, he said, "It isn't glamorous work like being the raven of a fey king, but it's honest and I'm desperate." He hesitated, then continued, "And I suppose, all things considered and laying all my cards on the table, I have a lady friend. She's not a Madam, not yet, but she's agreed to marry this old bachelor if I procure a white raven. She's a little too keen on status, but otherwise, a sweet brownie to whom I could happily see myself wedded."

Everyone held their breath waiting for Skorri's answer. "Two little ones?" he asked.

"Yes. My daughter and grandsons mean everything to me. My daughter was just about to earn her Madam when her husband died. I need to know they're safe, and I can't leave my post without forfeiting my Master. I need to retain my Master if I am to support them."

"The elves wouldn't grant you leave?" Filip asked, frowning. "You don't earn holidays?"

"It doesn't work like that," said Henrik. "It's the magic of the mastery, it's tied to brownie and also to place."

"How was Madam Brown able to join us?"

"Her mastery was breaking down," Aleks guessed. "We just didn't see it collapse because the time she had spent away from her home hadn't been that long."

Henrik clasped his hands together and stared at them, lost in thought. "Yes, I think you are correct. She could have bound herself to my father and Elleken. If she had, her mastery would've transferred."

Geirr hummed, "But she returned home before then, so that didn't happen."

"You're right," agreed Aleks.

"If you leave, you lose your magic?" Zaria asked, looking toward the brownie.

"It's not quite like that, either," said Master Brown. "The explanation is difficult, but suffice it to say, not knowing when or where I would find my family, that by the time I reached them, I wouldn't be able to help them. My magical stores would be depleted and without hope of refilling."

Christoffer frowned at Master Brown. "If my mother hadn't heard from me, I can tell you the last thing she'd do is wait three years to find me. She was at Zaria's door within hours of my disappearance. Why wait for a white raven? Why not send another in your place?"

Master Brown stared solemnly at him. "And risk my daughter's chances at mastery? The appearance of an anxious worried parent would've destroyed any shred of a chance she had to gain one. Besides, who would help a brownie? Or more specifically, me? I'm not the most likeable of brownies. I'm crotchety and set in my ways. I curse outsiders and disruption to my routine."

"And yet, he has a lady friend," murmured Christoffer still a little shocked. "Wouldn't she go and fetch them for you? You said she didn't have her Madam yet."

"She's earning one," Master Brown said sharply. "She can't leave her intended post anymore than I can leave mine. It is not her child or her grandchildren."

"She doesn't sound like a winner to me," he mumbled under his breath, feeling bad for Master Brown's romantic interests.

"Would you bring your grandsons here?" asked Skorri, watching from his perch, his keen eyes tracking every movement.

Master Brown hesitated afraid that his answer would drive away the raven. "That is my plan. I am going to raise them until my daughter can work through her grief and earn her Madam."

Skorri nibbled on a toe, deliberating. They all held their breath wondering what he would say in the face of Master Brown's plight.

"Oh, out with it," cried Airi, impatient. "What do you say?"

Clearing his throat, Skorri croaked. "I say yes."

Chapter Eight: A New Mission

Master Brown toppled off his chair with a squeak of surprise. "Truly, Master Raven? Will you truly agree to be my white raven?"

Skorri hopped and cawed. "Your story of woe is not something I could ignore. I am a feeling creature."

"Color me amazed," whispered Christoffer in Geirr's ear, drawing a quick bark of laughter.

Skorri glared at them and cleared his throat pompously. "I agree to stay and help you locate them. If I like your grandsons I may stay permanently, but if they're horrible little ogres with a mind to pull tailfeathers, then I'm out."

Master Brown's eyes misted in relief. He scrubbed them, then held out a small hand to the Elleken prince. "Thank you, Stag Lord. Even if it is just this much and not forever, consider the trade completed. I am satisfied."

"I would've helped you search for them, Master Brown," said Henrik looking stricken, reluctant to seal the trade out of guilt.

"The ellefolken prince spending his days looking for my family?" Master Brown eyed him skeptically. "How would you have found them? Are you as capable as a white raven?"

"He isn't," said Skorri, chucking and cawing.

Henrik frowned, playing with a strap on his bag. "It is true that I don't possess skills to match the raven, but I would've asked my friends for help. Aleks is an excellent navigator. Maybe you could've reunited with your family already."

Master Brown dropped his hand and glanced at Aleks, pinning him in place with his gaze. "Perhaps. He's no longer disowned I hear, but he was the last time we met. I would not have trusted him to handle my affairs."

"Uh guys," Aleks said clearing his throat. "I am still in the room. Can you see me?"

"Dunderhead," scoffed Skorri.

"Stuff it," muttered Airi, sleepily, nestling in and tucking her head. "He's my dunderhead."

"Ah, hey, come on now," Aleks whined.

Christoffer whispered consolingly, "At least she's the only one allowed to call you dunderhead."

"That's not a comfort," he said. He shook a finger at her. "Don't call me a dunderhead."

"Only when you are," she said sweetly. "Nap time. Night. Night."

Grinning at Aleks' raven, Christoffer gave her a thumbs up. "You and Saskia keep him on his toes."

"Really? You're supposed to be on my side," Aleks said, nearly throwing a pillow, but then thinking twice.

"Boys," Zaria cut in with exasperated fondness. "Master Brown, please know that we all regret not knowing why you needed Skorri."

"Would it have made you come here faster had you known?"

Her answering smile was faint. "I could only hope it would've."

"I should have mentioned it to you," he conceded, before fiddling with the teapot. "Does anyone want more tea? My teapot never gets cold while there is liquid in it, so it is still fresh."

"Oh, like the teapot in Granny's?" asked Filip, reaching over with his cup.

Geirr held a hand over the cup to halt Master Brown. "Her teapot brewed a perfect cup of tea, including one of poison, if you recall."

Master Brown moved Geirr's hand aside and poured the tea anyway, despite his disgruntled expression. "That was her teapot, not mine."

"Don't be rude," Zaria admonished gently.

Aleks stood his ground. "Her shop has as many defective trinkets as it does treasures," he reminded them.

"Are both teapots made from brownie magic?" asked Filip, accepting the cup of tea this time.

"Yes. You will find most brownies charm many household items to be more useful. Farming equipment, too, for that matter. Each piece is unique to the brownie who cast the charm. If you can sense magic, you may be able to detect a sheen of cobalt blue around the edges of the teapot. That is my signature color."

"Kind of like how Zaria's is purple?" asked Christoffer, leaning forward to examine the teapot. He didn't see any cobalt blue, just its ordinary cream and blue ceramic design.

Master Brown nodded. "Yes. Sorceress magic always has a purple sheen to it."

Zaria pressed him further. "I've seen my mother's magic; it has been many colors," she said, curious if he had an explanation.

"Indeed, she's spent countless years perfecting various spells, but her strongest magic will always be purple."

"Does a dwarf's magic cast a color?" asked Zaria, the first of them to find a way toward their ultimate goal of completing Queen Helena's command to restore the Drakeland Sword. She tried desperately to appear nonchalant.

"It does," Master Brown revealed. "However, it's far more muted due to the ores they use. One metal in particular has its own magic, which makes it more difficult to detect the presence of outside magics."

"Does the magic in the metal mask the dwarf's magical signature?" Geirr asked.

"A truly talented smith's magic will seep out of the metal itself regardless of the material worked. It can't be turned off, just like yours can't be. Not everyone can see it, of course, that's just how magic is. If you don't hone your ability to sense it you might never detect more than the strongest of magics on an object."

"One time I was supposed to detect magic in a piece of rope," Zaria said. "It didn't go over very well. I wasn't able to see anything. I think I embarrassed myself because I tried to detect magic by my other senses."

"She sniffed it," Filip explained at the brownie's confused look.

Master Brown chuckled. "That would have been a funny sight. No, magic is not actually detected by your normal senses, not even your eyesight. You can, however, see magic with your eyes when it's actively cast. But afterwards, spelled magic woven into objects or enchantments are detected with 'mage sight.' What is metaphysical can't be detected by something physical. They're too polar opposite."

"Magic detects magic," Zaria said.

"Precisely," said Master Brown.

"Can you tell us, is the stargazer dwarf-made?" Aleks asked, pulling it out of his pocket and handing it to the brownie.

Master Brown peered at it, pressing an eye against one or two of the stars. He then held it away from his face, commenting, "It's uncomfortably hot to the touch. How long has it been running?"

Aleks took the stargazer back and clasped it loosely between his palms. "I'm not entirely sure, a fair few days," he said noncommittedly.

"*Harrumph*," Master Brown said, busily packing away their tea and snacks. "It's not like I want it; or, like it matters to me how long you run that thing. It only works on mundanes."

"We didn't mean to offend," Henrik said, soothingly as Aleks hastily stowed the stargazer away.

"Right," agreed the fey king. "I tend to be more circumspect than the occasion warrants, but I really haven't been paying attention. At least a week and a half. Do you mind telling us more about the stargazer? Is it dwarf-made?"

"It is," Master Brown said testily. "Why?"

Aleks scrubbed his hand through his hair. "We were hoping to get—"

"Weapons," Zaria blurted.

"Weapons?" Master Brown asked, skeptically.

Behind him, Christoffer mouthed, "Weapons?"

She stuck out her tongue at him before turning back to the brownie. "There's another dragon war on the horizon and we're going to need to stockpile. The stargazer is the best dwarf-crafted item we've encountered."

Master Brown raised an eyebrow and canted his head to take her in. "Curious that the stargazer received that distinction, and not the Drakeland Sword."

Abashed, Zaria immediately backpedaled. "Well, I mean of course except for the Drakeland Sword."

"But that's one of a kind, am I right?" Christoffer cut in, saving her. "It's not like we could find a weaponsmith of such a high caliber."

"It is unlikely," agreed Master Brown, looking less suspicious. "That sword is a gift of magic and skill you're not likely to cross again until a true prodigy comes around."

"Which leads us back to the stargazer," Filip said. "If you knew who made it…"

"Then we can give that dwarf and his shop our custom," Henrik picked up smoothly.

Master Brown tugged on his chin hairs thoughtfully. "I believe the dwarf who made that is dead."

"Oh no," said Zaria. "What will we do now? We weren't expecting the smithy to be lost to us."

"That's true," Geirr said. "It seems like everyone lives nearly a millennium around these parts."

"Must be nice," Christoffer sighed.

"It comes with responsibilities and a tree form," Henrik said lightly.

"Speak for yourself," Aleks said, laughing lightly. "Mine comes with a fox form."

"I don't ever want to think of us not being together and being best friends," Zaria said, shutting down their side conversation.

Filip dropped a kiss on the top of her crown. "Same."

"Fear not, Princess," Master Brown said taking her hand in his. "I think I can help you. The stargazer is a truly ancient artifact, but its magic reminds me of someone alive now."

"Who?" asked Christoffer eagerly, leaning forward.

"May I see it again?" he asked Aleks, and the fey king fished it out of his pocket. Master Brown closed his eyes and concentrated. "The Master Gyllenhammar," he said slowly, sounding out each syllable. "Yes, the magic is reminiscent of that dwarf."

"Who's that?" asked Filip, draining his teacup and setting it aside.

"She's the head smith over all the guilds –" Henrik started.

"One might say she's the Golden Hammer, eh?" Christoffer said, jabbing an elbow into Geirr's side.

Geirr cuffed him on the back of the head. "Hush, you. The grownups are talking."

"That's real hurtful, man," Christoffer pouted.

"You'll grow out of it," Geirr teased.

"Oh, ouch. That was pretty good," he acknowledged. They turned their attention to the conversation that had continued without them.

"Aumak is a good friend of mine," Master Brown said, directing his words to Zaria. "She would help you… maybe."

"What did we miss?" Geirr asked Filip.

Filip whispered, "This Aumak is the Master Gyllenhammar's granddaughter. She and Master Brown know each other from before his mastery. They grew up together or something."

"Can you provide us an introduction?" the fey king asked, setting his teacup aside.

"She lives in an offshoot of the mine system in Malmdor."

"We're acquainted with that region," Zaria assured him. "Is she near the sunken palace?"

"Not far from there," he said. "Are you sure you need the Master Gyllenhammar? Aumak and her grandmother aren't close. Not since Aumak's accident in the forge. I'm not sure how much an introduction to my friend can help you."

"Are they estranged?"

"No," he hedged, fidgeting. "But like I said they're not close. When Aumak lost her hand saving a weather-wyvern from an explosion, her grandmother banished her from the guilds."

"So not exactly on friendly terms," Christoffer said.

"That sounds like an understatement," said Geirr.

"No, not on friendly terms. Aumak has resented her grandmother ever since. The guilds are where you make a name for yourself, you see."

Henrik persisted, "An introduction might still prove useful."

"Let me get that for you." Master Brown collected their cups and saucers with a wave of his hand and left the room, returning up the stairs.

Zaria settled back against Filip and tucked her feet to the side. He wrapped an arm around her and chaffed her arm, warming her up. She sighed. "That feels nice."

"I'm going to check on Defender," Christoffer said, standing up. "Does anyone have any leftover snacks that I can give him? I doubt he'll be happy swallowing fireflies even if they are protein."

"I have some dried meat and bread," Henrik said. "It should be fresh." He dug into his bag and handed him a couple of wrapped packages.

Christoffer waved to the group. "Thanks. I'll be right back."

He left Master Brown's home, exiting through the metallic door. Outside, he scanned the opening for the border collie. The muted glow from the twinkling fireflies kept the cave from true darkness, but the faint light strained the eyes. Turning left and right Christoffer looked for his dog but didn't spy him in the gloom.

Raising a hand to his mouth, he shouted, "Defender. Here boy. I have dinner."

He heard a distant woof and turned expectantly toward the sound. Defender barked again, announcing another's presence. Suddenly a bright light flared and Christoffer forced his gaze aside, blocking the light with his hand.

"Hey, now," he shouted.

"Oh, sorry," said a deep voice with rich overtones like dark chocolate. "Does the dog belong to you? He's very friendly."

Christoffer recognized that voice and relaxed. "He doesn't have a lick of sense," he complained.

"Aw, don't say that," protested Falkor, crossing the distance with Defender trotting happily at his heels. "Wolves love me, so why wouldn't he? He's a handsome mutt."

"Are you here by yourself?" Christoffer asked, shaking the mountain-troll's hand in greeting.

The tall, brawny troll towered over him like a running back. If he hadn't met giants, Christoffer would be tempted to call him as tall as one. Mountain-trolls prized themselves on their size and picked their leaders because of it, so comparing him to a giant was a compliment.

Dark slashing eyebrows punctuated his rugged face, which lit up with joy at seeing Christoffer. Clapping him heartily on the back, Falkor toppled him sideways without so much as a by-your-leave. Before Christoffer could pick himself up, the teenage troll did so single-handedly and dusted him off.

"I'm on patrol with the guys," Falkor said lightheartedly. "Regnor and Modolf are on the other side of the illusion wall. I came this way to investigate some snuffling sounds."

"That must've been Defender," Christoffer surmised.

"It's great to run into you. I was expecting something less pleasant."

"Oh?" asked Christoffer. "There seems to be a lot of that around Gloomwood these days. We ran into a hag, banshees, and an ogre above ground."

"We still find the odd one of those around from Jorkden's days, but no, we've actually had some run-ins with goblins of all things. Can't walk a dozen paces it seems without stumbling across one by the river."

"Olaf was having trouble with them earlier," Christoffer said. "Although, I suppose I need to call them Olebjørn."

"Them?" questioned Falkor, canting his head and looking down at him inquisitively.

"Bjarke joined Olaf and they became a two-headed troll a few days back."

Falkor's eyes bulged outwards. "They did what?"

Christoffer grinned. "Pretty wild, right?"

"Never in my life did I expect to see that river-troll do something like that. He always seemed so tough. What made them do it?"

"The Glomma was under attack from a dragon. Olaf couldn't ignore the signs anymore and when a kraken attacked Bjarke, their combined powers took it down." He didn't mention that they joined in two-headed form after defeating the kraken.

Falkor's eyes, which had relaxed, bulged again in disbelief. "You're telling me you've all seen a kraken? And survived? With all your limbs intact?"

"It was the biggest bloody crab I've ever seen," Christoffer said. "Tasted great, too."

"What's taking you so long, Falkor?" a growly voice reverberated down the cavern.

"I ran into Christoffer, you remember him? He's been telling me the most incredible stories."

A lean, long-limbed troll with a mountain of hair like a rock star appeared carrying a lantern. "No goblins?"

"None that I've seen. Modolf, get over here and bring Regnor."

"Hold your bears," Regnor groused, his loud voice drowning out the sound of the water.

His needle-sharp tail whipped through the air and stole the lantern from Modolf. He held it aloft, bringing Falkor and Christoffer into the circle of light. Regnor looked like a ruffian in pants with holes torn at the knee and a bulky leather jacket.

Squinting at them, Christoffer waved hello just as the door to Master Brown's home opened, spilling out his friends one by one. Filip, Aleks, and Geirr noticed their visitors immediately, but Zaria and Henrik were bidding goodbye to the brownie, thanking him for his note of introduction to Aumak.

Just like that, without hearing a word, he knew with a simple exchange of paper and hands the quest to escort Skorri to the brownie was completed, old debts paid off, and honor upheld. A new mission immediately replaced the old challenge – as it should with any good heroic adventure. Their new task would have them cross realms, conduct business, and craft swords.

First, they must meet this Aumak and discover more about dwarvish metallurgy, all in hopes of seeing the Master Gyllenhammar and getting the Drakeland Sword restored to its former glory. Each step, one step closer to that penultimate goal.

Master Brown spied the trolls and glowered. Henrik looked up from fastening his golden-antlered cloak and waved. Zaria turned around noticing their company for the first time.

"Oh," she said, startled. "Hi!" The words were bright, but then she peered anxiously around them. "Kanutte isn't here with you, is she?

"The elders don't let her and Falkor patrol together," teased Modolf. "Because not much patrolling gets done if you know what I mean."

"I don't see the elders letting you patrol with Gisken."

"My girlfriend and I are a right sight better than you two lovebirds. We at least haven't been caught by Grizzle. How much sucking face were you doing to miss that old crone sneaking up on you?"

Falkor's ears heated and he clenched his fists. His tail lashed tensely side to side.

"Don't be causing any fights," Master Brown warned tetchily, sensing trouble. "I don't want to be spending weeks repairing the water wheel. Go on and get out of here."

"Good bye Master Brown. Bye Skorri!" Christoffer called out.

A wry caw came from inside the brownie's home. "Not sorry!"

Christoffer laughed, feeling like he'd actually miss that sour-faced white raven after all. He'd always felt close to those with a sense of humor, and the messenger bird, despite all odds, had located one in the end.

Finding a new home and a new place in the world did wonders to one's disposition. He hoped the two helped each other and forged a new little family.

"Good luck finding your family," he said, reaching out to shake the brownie's hand.

"Thank you," he said. "Now, be gone. We have much to plan."

"All right," Christoffer said affably, understanding the small creature's desire to focus on the larger problem of what comes next. He waved. "We're leaving."

"You're friendly with that brownie," Modolf said gruffly, falling into step beside Christoffer.

"I didn't like him at first, but he's all right. A little uptight, but not a bad sort," he said.

Modolf made a face. "He's always cussing us out. Treats us like common hoodlums."

"Probably because of all the pranks we pulled on him," said Regnor. "Remember when we put soap suds in the waterfall? Bubbles reached the ceiling."

"That was the most benign trick," Falkor said, shaking his head. "The worst they ever pulled – well, let's just say they once put mermaid spawn in the lake."

"That doesn't seem too awful," said Geirr. "I mean it doesn't seem smart, but why is that the worst prank?"

"When one of the little monsters hatched there was nothing to eat so after it cannibalized its siblings it nearly got Master Brown who hadn't known it was there until it was almost too late."

"I'm sorry I asked," Geirr said, grimacing.

"Yeah," Regnor said, looking chagrinned. "That was pretty bad of us. Mother tanned my hide for that one."

"It was a mess to clean up," Modolf said, shuddering.

Zaria looked queasy. "I can only imagine."

"I'd rather not," said Filip, shaking his head. "I've had to swim in a swarm of them and –"

"I swear you make these stories up," Falkor complained. "It's either that or we do not go on any exciting adventures. The Wild Hunt was supposed to bring us glory, but it's like going to a petting zoo."

Christoffer clapped him on the back. "Don't beat yourselves up. Our journeys are fraught with danger, sure, but what tale isn't when dragons are involved? You've had plenty of wild tales, too."

Falkor looked disgusted. "You mean Zorka does. She got to join you in Niffleheim, while we were stuck here in Trolgar. Kanutte still refuses to be in the same room when she's talking about the Ravagers."

"It's only because it's your kingdom and your home that you don't see how marvelous your own story is," Zaria said kindly. "You led revolts, protected those who couldn't protect themselves, and were integral in overthrowing a false king and his henchmen."

They'd reached the tunnel that led back to the main corridor. Lining up single file the group headed through the narrow stone hallway and back to the illusion wall. One by one they slipped around its edge like nimble minnows.

"What's the point of the wall if you know where it is?" asked Aleks. "I thought it was hidden so non-trolls could pass through or escape as needed."

"It is hidden," said Regnor. At the fey king's dubious look, he raised his hands in supplication. "Relax. It's all because of my uncle Yorgish. I told you before, he has a lady-elf friend."

"They've been together for many years," added Modolf. "Personally, I don't get it. She's too tiny for my tastes, but I guess he likes her, so that's all that matters."

The further they went, the cooler the passageway became, until without quite knowing how it happened, Christoffer was shivering. Glancing at the others he saw their breath fog in the air, hanging around like little clouds of smoke and vapor and wreathing around their heads. He assumed it was the same for him, but he couldn't see it. Gooseflesh prickled down his arms and only Defender's close proximity kept his legs from breaking out.

Zaria conjured torches, which she then lit with purple fire. The blazes danced and sputtered in the wind, blowing through the tunnel. He was careful to protect his, shielding it with his body, eager to absorb any warmth. The flames' heat licked his face, bringing relief.

"Thanks," Filip said when she handed him his and he held it close. "I was freezing."

"Be careful," she warned him. "Don't burn your eyebrows off."

"So, besides mermaids, krakens, two-headed trolls, and white ravens, what else has been going on?" asked Falkor, waving his torch around.

"Two-headed trolls!?" bellowed Modolf and Regnor together. "Hold up. Why are we just now hearing about this?"

Chapter Nine: Grizzle's Tale

The bow-legged teen held up a hand to stop them. "Just wait until my godmother hears about this. She'll have more to say."

Modolf let out a grumbly laugh. "Of course, she will; she's Trolgar's historian."

"When was the last time this has happened?" asked Regnor, whipping his tail back and forth in excitement.

Falkor scratched his head, "I don't know. Maybe when a Chicken-Hearted and a Fumble-Footed teamed up to become a Lionhearted?"

Regnor shook his head vehemently, "No way. That is just a boogeyman tale our mothers tell us to make us behave."

Modolf nodded. "But if you ask them, well, the Lionhearted would never refute it. Makes them look good to have that tale bandied about to all the youngsters to scare them."

"Grizzle will know. We can ask her when we see her," Falkor said, settling the matter for now.

"You'll have to give her the whole story," Modolf grinned wolfishly. "I, for one, can't wait. That and she'll give us gløgg if we sweet-talk her. Ever since the Glomma froze over, I've been in a mood for something warm to drink."

Regnor slapped his head. "We're such idiots!" he cried.

Zaria looked at him in alarm. "What?"

He pointed to the ghostly white river that lay at the bottom of the incline. "The river – two-headed trolls!"

"You think that's why it froze early?" Aleks asked.

Falkor's eyes lit up. "It has to be. That makes much more sense than thinking what we thought."

Regnor jabbed his tail at Aleks. "At first, we wondered if Olaf was up to his old tricks, testing our defenses, what with the goblins littered about down here like flies on winter-wyvern dung."

"But we couldn't understand why'd he'd do it," said the burly troll, gesticulating. "Not after being free of Koll's influence. He'd seemed like a changed troll."

"I mean, we knew it could've been another dragon," said Modolf as they stepped out onto the ice. "But how likely is that?"

"Try extremely likely," said Geirr, arms pinwheeling as he skidded the first few steps on the frozen subterranean river. "We know another one is loose."

"We just don't know which one it is," said Henrik. "I have my suspicions, but I'm not yet prepared to voice them."

"Oh, come now," Christoffer whined. "You can't just say something like that and not follow it up."

"Well, who do you think it is?" asked Henrik.

"Me?" he asked, surprised. "I don't know the names of more than five dragons. How could I begin to guess?"

"You truly can't?" Henrik pressed and he shook his head. The Stag Lord frowned in disappointment. "It may become clearer in time."

Aleks eyed the Stag Lord, speculation in his brown-eyed gaze. "Are you thinking it's –"

"It makes sense, doesn't it?" he asked.

The fey king nodded, slow in thought. "What do you think comes next?"

"Next is simple," said Henrik. "Next is one step and then another."

"To the witch?" asked Zaria.

"Hang on, now," Christoffer interrupted. "Let's not be too hasty. We were invited to hang out with our trolden friends."

Geirr gave a thumbs up. "I think that's smarter. We can't be sure how quickly Olebjørn can spread the word and by sticking around we can help Queen Helena and them."

Falkor rubbed his hands together. "Oh, good, I'm glad you six can join us."

Regnor scratched his backside. "I still want to know which dragon you lot think it is."

"We know significantly more than five dragons' names," said Modolf. He counted on his fingers. "There's Egil, the last of the three original brothers; Bodvar and Vigrun, the twins; Skade, a shrewd and conniving enemy if there ever was one, very proficient at revenge; Kefas, the dragon of hate whose malice will curl your tail at a hundred leagues; Sollaug, the demoralizer, just the idea of having to stand in front of her could put you in a tailspin; Narfi, the selfish, petty one; Greip the stirrer of envy, whose greed and gluttony are unmatched; Ginna the deceiver; Logi whose torturous deeds with fire can give you nightmares worse than any mare—"

"You've run out of fingers," noted Falkor drily as they reached the outskirts of the city of Trolgar. "Before you take off your boots and kill us dead from the smell, let's stop there."

"There are so many dragons," Zaria fretted, her brow knit with worry. "Even if we stop this one, another will take its place."

"Be that as it may, Princess," Henrik said. "We still fight."

He sounded so much like Hector that Zaria's eyes smarted.

"Every day," added Aleks, noticing and lending comfort. "Because fighting evil brings hope."

"Hope that it will end," said Filip, hugging her close and guiding her carefully off the icy river.

"You've showed us it could," Christoffer said meaningfully, before turning and looking at his fey friend. "Aleks too, when he followed your lead."

Regnor clapped Aleks on the shoulder, steering him to the side. "Just how did you do it? Zaria had her sorceress powers, so we thought that was the secret to her success, but you're just a fey. How did you do it? Did you use the Drakeland Sword?"

Aleks shook his head and said, "I used one of the daggers from the Gjöll."

"Wait, but you're the fey king! How did you not lose your magic when you touched it?" Modolf asked, his brow furrowing tightly.

"Airi, here, saved me," Aleks admitted. "Without her quick thinking I'd have lost all my magic and maybe even my life."

"Wow," the trolls said, looking admiringly at his raven as she rode on his shoulder.

She preened under the attention and nibbled on a claw. "It was nothing," she said modestly, knocking softly in her throat.

They trudged along the low-lying ground, past the barn full of reindeer, and past the sheep and cattle pens. Wolves prowled about like sheepdogs tracking everything with their keen eyes. A few trolden waved as the motley group strolled up through the outer edges and onto the busier streets.

Towering, spindly stalagmites formed the city, creating a forest-like space on the ground. Along the ceiling, mirrors were used to cast sunlight around the cavern to the streets below. At night, great fires were lit in large braziers to keep the city from falling into shadow.

It felt good to roam the streets and not be under threat of the Wild Hunt, a first. Christoffer could look at everything to his heart's content. He called out greetings to the young troll kids kicking and hitting a ball amongst themselves. They stared openly in shock at the sight of humans until one with short little tusks and pigtails bounded over and dragged him into their group.

The game they were playing was a mix of hacky-sack meets four square, but with three teams of six. They explained the rules to him, describing penalties and rewards. Per team, the ranks, in order, were: thrall, karl, warrior, berserker, jarl, and king. You fought for your rank on your team and also against the other teams for victory points.

"What's it called?" Christoffer asked the little girl.

She replied in a sweet, little, innocent voice, "Skull Toss." Her eyes twinkled mischievously waiting for his response.

That's when Christoffer realized the ball in question was somewhat oddly shaped. He laughed uncomfortably. "Not a human skull, though, right?"

Her knowing, amused gaze caused him to shiver.

"That's just what the kids call it," Regnor said, chortling. "Don't be fooled. It's Castle Fortitude, which is a modern version of Gut Check. That one was more about sucker-punching everyone and not barfing up a lung."

"Oh, okay. So… just checking, there's a referee to call penalties for unnecessary or overly rough physical contact, right?" Christoffer asked, reluctantly taking the ball.

Regnor smirked, "If you need one against these little tykes, we can perform that office."

"Just don't aim for my face," he warned the kids, and joined the game in the lowest spot for his team as the thrall.

There were a lot of flying knees and elbows and some well-placed spikes and tusks, but Christoffer held his own and advanced to the third spot. His team lost in the end, but the game was more fun than he'd expected.

For the next round, Zaria and Geirr were coerced by several pairs of big rounded eyes and oversized tusks. They joined Christoffer's team taking the two bottom ranks, which bumped Christoffer's starting position up to warrior. They lost spectacularly, making for a short round.

The kids really went wild when Falkor and Regnor decided to play a third round. They looked to the older teen trolls with wide-eyes and no small amount of hero worship. Disentangling from them was hard to do, but the kids eventually, reluctantly, let them go after extracting the promise of a rematch.

"They love you," Zaria said admiringly.

Modolf grinned and jogged backwards so he could watch her. "It's because they ran the varsity league in school and were champions. Of course, now that we're adults we'll form our own club, maybe join an intermural league."

"Here we are," Falkor said, stopping Modolf from walking too far by catching the other troll's ankle with his tail.

They stood outside one of the many stalagmites in this tighter section of the city. The bases of all the buildings melded at the bottom in one thick interconnected chunk. Wide balconies above ran the length of each column. At first glance, Christoffer thought they'd be easy to scale. Nothing like the daring jumps they had to make from the palace to its nearest neighbor during their last visit.

The burly troll opened the thick-planked oak door on the middle house and poked his head inside. "Grizzy, are you home?" he called inside.

"Is that you, my favorite godson?" a creaky voice called out.

"I brought friends, Grizzy. They've got something you need to hear."

"Come in, come in," she said, reaching the door and opening it wide.

An ancient looking troll with a wrinkly face, hoary chin, and yellowed tusks met them. Grizzle leaned on a cane and scratched her large belly, her eyes glittering with interest as Falkor revealed just who his friends were. She cackled in delight.

"Why, if it isn't the Sorceress Princess, Stag Lord, and Raven King? What news do you have to share?"

"Ones you wouldn't believe," said Falkor, "Except it's them telling it."

They trooped into her home; the nine of them, plus Defender and Airi, squishing into the large ovalish living room. It looked vastly different from the other troll home that Christoffer had seen. The center of the room held a triangular fireplace, with a skinny metal chimney soaring upwards through the floors. It was lit and pumped out heat into the chilly room.

Stairs wrapped around the entire space until they met the floor above and continued on. She had plush rugs covering the floor and six, large, well-made, wooden chairs with plump cushions in bright colors filling the space, circling the fireplace. Square tables dotted the spaces between the chairs and were piled high with towering tomes of trollish tales.

The trolls all claimed a seat, leaving two chairs for the rest of them. Christoffer sat in one with Aleks and Henrik perching on the arms like bookends. Zaria and Filip squished into the last one with Geirr resting his hip against their armrest. Defender sprawled out in front of the fire and instantly started snoring.

Grizzle snapped her fingers and an elderly brownie appeared in a bulky, fur-lined tunic carrying mugs of steaming liquid.

"Yum! Gløgg," Modolf said appreciatively, accepting a heavy ceramic mug and sipping it eagerly.

When everyone held a mug and the brownie disappeared, Falkor leaned forward, bracing his elbows on his knees. "Grizzy, you need to hear what they have to say. It's important. King Kafirr will want to know too, but I knew you'd want to hear it first from them."

She gulped down her gløgg, belched and grinned. Waving a hand, she encouraged, "Well, do go on. Tell me everything."

At the conclusion, she whistled. "I never thought we'd see the day when those stodgy, righteous, river-trolls would merge into a two-headed troll. The power they wield together is truly legendary. You say they took down a kraken. Minimal casualties? You're right Falkor, King Kafirr will need to be informed."

"They didn't team up to fight the mountain-trolls," Zaria inserted hastily.

"True, they had bigger fish to fry," Grizzle said, tapping her cane on the floor.

"Good one," Christoffer blurted out. When the others looked at him blankly, he tried to explain. "You know, because they took down the kraken and we ate it? Some of it fried? Oh, never mind."

"Ha," said Geirr.

Christoffer scoffed, rolling his eyes. "Comedy peons."

He ran his finger along the spines of the books near him. The colorful titles jumped out at him – *The Histories of the Iron-Bellied Kings in Eight Parts, Volume Two*; *Bridge to Wolf Hall*; *The River Wife*; *The First Hunt: Origin of the Wild Hunt*; *A Troll's Heart: Is it Made of Stone?*; *Squish, Squish: A Modern Guide to Meat Sourcing and Preparation*. There seemed to be a range of non-fiction and fiction among the titles. Grizzle's house felt much like a library, at least until she spat and it sizzled in the fire, making him jump.

"Tell them about the Lionhearted," encouraged Regnor, sprawling out in his chair.

"The Tale of the First Lionhearted," she said, leaning back and closing her eyes resting her hands on her large belly. "Some say it's myth, others say it's true."

"But you believe it's true," Regnor said, eyes bright with enthusiasm.

She cracked open an eyelid, giving him the stink eye. "Are you going to keep interrupting?"

"No, ma'am."

She snorted, closed her eye, and began. *"Back when the land was untamed, wild, and covered in mist… when dragons still roamed free and terrorized the countryside, there was a small human village called Oakland in the great woods to the south. The village lay near several forest-troll homesteads and paid danegeld to the trolls to live in peace.*

"In the village there was a mighty smith who made many trinkets and tools for the humans. He was the cleverest and most devious man in the village and he was tired of giving the best of his wares to the trolls. He knew all the trolls that lay in the woods around his smithy by sight.

"He often saw, through the smoke and soot of his forge, the happenings in the trees. He knew not all trolls were equal in power or status and they failed to keep their squabbles to themselves. He saw which ones got last pick of his treasures each year; those who seemed poorer than the others. They were not as tall, or strong, or powerful. He thought they might resent the bigger trolls the way he did.

"One day, after many long weeks spent in contemplation, he set aside his tools and gathered his courage. After placing a sign on his door for his absence, he strolled out of the village and into the forest heading toward the first of two trolls with whom he'd decided to strike a bargain.

"The yard of this one was filled with many chickens. Here was the homestead of a troll so ridiculed by trolden society that his true name was forgotten. His house was dubbed the Chickenhearted, for this troll was the worst sort of coward.

"In fact, when the smith arrived at his home, Chikenhearted refused to come outside for fear, but he listened with an attentive ear to the things the smith said. He promised Chickenhearted the opportunity for great power if the troll would meet him in three days' time behind his smithy to obtain a newly forged spear. Chickenhearted promised to be there, for the lure of power is not one a troll can easily shake, even if a human offers it, and even if the troll in question is as fearful as a chicken in the presence of a fox.

"The next day the smith set out in the opposite direction and found a humble homestead overrun with cats. Pussyfooted lived there and he was incapable of commitment, never siding with anyone and therefore never having anyone on his side. He was weak in body, and weak-willed, and lived in fear of the bigger trolls who preyed on him and subjugated him as if he were human himself.

"When the smith told him of a way to reverse his fortunes from being the most despised to being the ruler of all, Pussyfooted could hardly believe it. When asked to come to the smith's forge in two days' time to receive a special axe, he didn't give an answer; but the smith was relying on his powers of persuasion to do the trick and ultimately convinced the troll to come.

"It took a day to travel home, and along the way, he told the other trolls of a new troll in the area. One said to be more powerful than any trolls alive. Well, the others did not take kindly to their territory being threatened and demanded to know where to find this new troll. The smith promised them if they arrived at the village on the day the danegeld was to be collected, the new troll would be there too, demanding its share.

"'We'll challenge him to a duel,' said the youngest troll.

"'If he defeats you, he won't defeat me,' said the oldest troll. 'I have more experience in duels.'

"'If he beats you both, I am bigger and stronger still,' said the third and mightiest of the trolls.

"Having stirred the ire of the remaining forest-trolls, the smith returned home and settled in to wait for Chickenhearted and Pussyfooted. When they arrived at the back of the smith's forge and spotted the other, they nearly fled. Neither was expecting to see another troll.

"'Wait,' said the smith. 'You have to hear what I heard from the other trolls after I left your homes.'

"Their curiosity piqued, they stayed and listened in horror at the thought of a new, stronger, mightier troll moving into the area. Chickenhearted fretted and Pussyfooted wrung his hands.

"'If only there was a way to combine forces,' cried the smith, which was a prevarication because he already knew of folktales about trolls with multiple heads.

"'There is a way,' one of them said warily.

"For these two trolls knew of such things themselves, but had never contemplated it, because cowards as they were, the other troll head would surely control them. As they eyed each other, a tempting, tantalizing question could clearly be seen going through each of their thoughts: 'What if I combined with another troll as cowardly as me? Would I then have the place of first head?' Their eyes gleaming, they looked to the other and struck a bargain, each hopeful to be the controlling and powerful, first head.

"They agreed that until this new troll was dealt with, they would join forces, become a two-headed troll, and fight together to lay claim to the surrounding forest and the village. The trolls who had bullied them would know their wrath as well. When they joined, the two's magic melded and doubled and their appearance changed drastically as their weaknesses disappeared. Together they became stronger, swifter, and self-assured.

"The smith praised them for their cleverness, saying they had done more for themselves than he could've, but he offered them the spear and axe from his shop as promised. Taking delight in their new strength, the two heads agreed on a new name for themselves. They were to be Lionhearted.

"When the other three forest-trolls arrived the next day, it was to find a new, two-headed troll they'd never seen before. Lionhearted challenged them to a duel, certain that with the smith's weapons, their newfound powers, and courage they could beat their long-time opponents and tormentors.

"One by one each of the bigger, stronger trolls fell. For they knew not who their opponent was while their opponent knew everything about them. The youngest died by the spear, too foolish to not realize that the spear, when wielded by a troll with enhanced magic, could actually pierce his thick hide. He ran right into it, in an attempt to wrest it from them.

"The second, the oldest and more experienced, was cautious in his approach, but had never had to face a two-headed attack. All previous fights he'd been in had been one vs one, not two vs one. Lionhearted easily crushed him, too, having the advantage of two heads to think and attack separately. While parrying one head and his weapon the other head got his unprotected flank.

"The last one, the meanest of the lot, fell to Lionhearted as easily as the others. He relied on his strength, and while having enough to take on ten or twenty men at once, he could not face a two-headed troll with the strength of thirty men. They broke his back clean in two.

"Lionhearted took the tusks from their defeated rivals and wore them like a bloody badge of honor. All the danegeld the two-headed troll had missed throughout the years was stripped clean from the defeated trolls' homesteads. Meanwhile, the smith gloried in his triumph and rose in stature amongst the village. He was ushered in as a jarl, praised for his cunning.

"The two-headed troll and the smith went their separate ways. That is, until the next year when danegeld was owed. The jarl-nee-smith refused, saying that without his help, Lionhearted would not be ruler of the forest. Of course, Lionhearted didn't like that one bit and threatened to destroy the village. They gave the smith one day to gather the danegeld or to face retribution.

"But the smith didn't worry. He was still as observant as he'd been a year before and noticed that the second head seemed upset with the first head. He remembered that the bargain struck last year was to end after they had secured their position in the forest.

"It seemed to the smith that the first head had reneged on the bargain, enjoying too much their combined power, which now was entirely at his disposal. For you must remember that while multi-headed trolls share greater power together than wield alone, one head is still stronger and can subjugate all the remaining heads and force them to do its bidding.

"On the following morning when danegeld was demanded, the smith presented Lionhearted with a new weapon. A gorgeous sword encrusted with jewels the size of quail eggs. The two heads fought over it and each pulled out their original weapon from the smith. Before the second head knew what was about, the first head had sliced their body in two halves with the axe. Crippled and in pain, the first head, which had survived the bloody *separation, missed the smith raising a hidden weapon and never saw the blow coming.*

"Thus ends this cautionary tale: be wary in whom you place your trust — should you ever need to be conjoined — and above all, never trust a human."

Christoffer clapped his hands. "Bravo, but the real lesson here is: do nothing half-assed. Don't you think?"

His friends groaned and Grizzle whacked his shins with a cane. "Don't be a smart aleck."

"Better that than a Chickenhearted," he returned with a laugh. "He lacked courage and intelligence."

"Or a Pussyfooted," added Geirr. "He lacked intelligence and honor."

"Or the smith," said Falkor. "While smart and sly, he lacked honor and morality, choosing to kill an unsuspecting opponent instead of fighting in a duel."

"Touché," Christoffer grinned.

Chapter Ten: The Witch's Prize

Grizzle let the party sleep in her home, but shooed her godson and his friends out the door. "I don't have space for you hooligans. Go see your girlfriends."

"Bye Grizzy," Falkor said, kissing her withered cheek. She patted him on the cheek and shoved him forcibly out the door.

"Bye Falkor!" Zaria called, waving. He held out a hand in return, before grabbing his friends and wrestling them down the streets.

Grizzle shut the door and eyed them all speculatively. "A dragon you say. Which one?"

"We haven't seen it," said Henrik. "Just the effects of its presence."

"So, it could be nothing, but you don't think it is," she said, her tail swishing contemplatively.

"Neither did Olaf and Bjarke."

"That's why they became Olebjørn."

"Precisely," Henrik said. "We need everyone to be on the lookout. Everyone must be ready. Queen Helena will be calling for aide once she figures out who is loose."

"Or free, if the dragon is no longer in the Under Realm," Grizzle said. "Increased goblin presence in places they're not normally seen, elves dead at their posts, giant tribes acting against their principles, a slumbering kraken suddenly awake, and a newly minted two-headed troll. It does appear something is going on beneath the surface of Norway. I'll have to consult Trolgar's palace library. Maybe I can figure out the dragon based on these clues."

"The great houses and the king will need to be informed," Aleks said.

"And they will be, but on the morrow. It is time to rest these old bones." Scratching her backside, she called again for the brownie. "Show these young people to where they can sleep."

"This way," the brownie beckoned nasally, indicating the stairs.

"Thank you, Master Brown," Filip said.

"Not a master," the brownie countered. "Just Ivan."

"What's your story?" he asked as they climbed to the next level.

"Freed from Autumn Court," Ivan said, glancing over at Aleks warily.

"That's great," the fey king said. "I meant it when I said anyone who wanted to leave should. Are you being treated well?"

"Yes," said Ivan. "I wanted to work in a library. Grizzle offered post. She is a troll, but she lets me tend to the books as I see fit."

"Good," said Aleks. "I am glad. Please let me, Saskia, Nori, or Sivert know if you require anything. We'll be happy to help you obtain your master if you wish it."

"I'll consider it," Ivan said, a hint of distrust in his voice. He stopped and gestured. "This is your room for the night. Do make yourselves at home."

They'd climbed two sets of stairs and the room they stood in now was much smaller than the living room. Folded blankets and heaps of pillows were piled in the center, next to the chimney stack that rose through the floor. They slung their bags onto the floor, dropping them where they stood.

"Bathroom?" Geirr asked, pulling his things from his pack. Ivan indicated the room above, and with a quiet thanks, their friend went upstairs.

Christoffer made a nest of blankets and unfurled his sleeping bag. Cracking a yawn, he flung himself down and snuggled in, preparing for sleep. Toenails clicked on the stone stairs and a low accusing woof moved the hairs next to his ear.

"Well, lay down, you big lug," he said, keeping his eyes closed. "You're the one who fell asleep next to the fire downstairs. It's not my fault you didn't wake up and join me sooner."

"Woof," Defender huffed, longsuffering, and circled, once, twice, thrice, four times and settled down into a snug warm ball.

It wasn't surprising that they slept like trolls that night, which is why Christoffer couldn't figure out what woke him. Was it a bad dream? He'd suffered from many of those in recent nights, ever since that hulder in the woods.

In the dark, he heard his friends breathing, one or two softly snoring. Defender's warm breath tickled his ear. Aurally, everything seemed fine, but he couldn't shake the lingering apprehension.

He sat up and peered into the gloom. At the center of the room, near their things, he saw movement. Standing quickly, he seized the fur cloak of the brownie and hauled him upright. "What's the meaning of this, Ivan?" he hissed.

Defender woke with a snort and Airi croaked in warning, lifting her head from under her wing. They stared at the struggling brownie in curiosity and suspicion. Ivan bit his hand and Christoffer cursed, flinging the brownie across the room.

"You feral little thing, what are you doing going through our stuff?" he shouted, waking the others.

Henrik just missed grabbing the brownie as it scuttled out of the room, racing down the stairs.

"Did he steal anything?" Filip asked, opening his pack and looking inside.

"Not that I saw," said Christoffer, nursing his hand. "He's got a nasty bite. Watch out."

"Still, we should all check," Zaria said, lighting the room with floating purple fireballs.

"You check for the thing Queen Helena has put in your charge," Geirr said. "It's the most important thing on us."

"I have my stargazer," said Aleks, checking his bag. "It's starting to feel like a miniature sun. It's so hot."

"We've been taxing it," Henrik said. "There may be a limit to what it can handle."

"It better last until the end of this adventure," Christoffer said drily. "You don't want to hear the howler my mother would send me."

"Your mother would need a white raven, not an owl, to reach you," Geirr said, laughing.

"She'd find one, believe me," Christoffer said. "She's capable of anything."

"Nothing's missing from my pack," said Filip, closing his bag. "Although everything smells like fish."

"I have the shield," said Christoffer, moving it aside and reaching for some gauze at the bottom of his pack.

Henrik nodded. "Good, we need that for the witch."

Zaria checked her bag. "I have the thing from my mother."

That meant the sword was safe, or at least its pieces. They all breathed a collective sigh of relief. Christoffer frowned at the empty stairwell. Just what had the brownie been looking for? Did Grizzle know about his thieving tendencies or did she order him to do it?

"Let's all just go back to sleep," Filip suggested, eyeing the stairs wearily. "I don't think Ivan will be back tonight."

"I suggest using your packs as your pillows for the remainder of the night," Henrik said, closing his up and folding his cloak on top of it.

"Maybe we also take watch shifts?" suggested Christoffer. "I'll go first."

They did, but even still, the rest of the night was fitful and they were glad when the new day arrived. After a wary breakfast, served by Ivan, in front of Grizzle, they were unsure what was going on. Were Ivan's actions sanctioned by Grizzle? Was the mountain-troll an enemy, or just her appalling brownie, or perhaps something else was going on?

None of them mentioned to Grizzle what the brownie had done out of an abundance of caution. With plans to execute and places to be they beat a hasty exit as soon as they could get away. When Christoffer glanced over his shoulder, he spotted Grizzle watching them from her doorway, fingering the hairs on her hoary chin contemplatively.

The group of friends left Trolgar without further incident and cut across Gloomwood Forest making quick work of the return trip to the home of the witch of the woods. The ogre, banshees, and hag were not to be seen, perhaps sleeping through the morning. They seemed more like nocturnal beings, or at least brunch buddies.

The witch's hidden realm appeared like magic out of the early morning mist. The turning trees fanned out like courtiers displaying their latest fashion plates. Ruby reds and mustard golds mingled and sighed in the breeze. On the ground a thick carpet of leaves crunched underfoot.

A single large tree, whose trunk sprawled equally upward and outward, stood at the center of the glade. A fanciful rosemåling design scrawled across its surface and a peeling Dutch door, its top half thrown wide open, beckoned. A glass bowl with a towel draped atop to hold flies at bay sat on the little sill.

As they traipsed up to the witch's door, a short female brownie appeared. Upon seeing them, Magga scowled. "Oh, it's you," she said frostily, picking up the bowl.

Christoffer grinned and pushed his way past the irritable creature, ignoring her huffiness. "It is me, indeed." He sang out, "Witch, we come bearing gifts!"

"No need to shout," she admonished, putting down the pestle and jar she'd been holding.

The witch pushed aside her project with its many bundles of dried, fragrant herbs. With a crooked finger, she beckoned him to drop his heavy burden on the table. He did so with a flourish and undid the latch on his backpack. Opening the bag, he shifted his dirty laundry out of the way and seized ahold of his treasure.

Giving a mighty tug, he pulled the svefnthorn from its housing and laid it beside her eager hands. She snatched it up and peered all around, taking in the oily patina. A wordless snap of her fingers brought Magga to her side with a little open jar of white odorless powder. The witch sprinkled it judiciously over the shield. She took the wet rag that Magga handed her and got to scrubbing.

"What is that?" he asked, leaning closer trying to see.

"Baking powder," she said toothily. The washcloth cut through the layer of grime like it was a hot knife going through butter.

Peering over her shoulder, he watched as a runic design was revealed. "Is it a svefnthorn?"

"It appears to be such. See this rune? It's for protection. That one is for water."

"What about those?" asked Filip, walking over with Aleks to join them at the counter. He leaned over and flicked at one of the other runes.

"These runes are for safety and indicate a great need. Altogether, it does appear to be a sleep thorn designed to protect one from a sea creature. Perhaps a water-wyvern or a kraken."

"Oddly enough, that's where I found this," said Christoffer, feeling pretty proud of his gutsy maneuver. "Inside a kraken's jaws."

The witch tsked, handing Christoffer the rag so he could continue to clean it. "Doesn't appear to have helped the poor sod who's shield this was. Is the kraken dead?"

"It is," said Henrik at the door. He wiped his feet and crossed the threshold. "If it hadn't been for Olaf and Bjarke joining forces I don't think we would've survived the encounter."

The witch's eyes lit up. "Oh ho, cousins and now brothers in arms."

"They're brothers in heads too," Christoffer said with a grin, trying to shock the witch.

"Two-headed?" she asked, her face crinkling in a toothy smile.

"It's not a bad idea for them to change their state and their name," Magga squeaked. "With a dragon loose, this could be the added protection they need to save their river."

"You are right," the witch agreed. "One can't be too cautious when one is facing a duplicitous being such as a dragon. The forest has been teeming and shifting as if a big quake were shaking its very foundations. Be alert at all times, children. The dragon is near."

"So, what do you think?" Christoffer pressed. "Better than some seashell, right?"

The witch rapped her knuckles on the counter. "It is, but it's of no use to me," she said.

He deflated at her dismissal. "It's not? Are you sure? I wrested it from the sea!"

"But the svefnthorn was not the first or even the second thing you lot pulled from the water."

"It's the only thing I got from the water," he said, running a finger in the groove of the old runes. "Was I supposed to bring you an oar? I completed a run of the oars, you know."

"Very brave," the witch said, with a motherly touch under his chin. "Grown men have lost their kneecaps to that, but no, I did not want an oar."

"What did you want?" Henrik asked, frowning.

Filip's eyes lit up. He wrestled with the opening of his bag. "She wanted what I took from the mermaids."

The witch straightened in anticipation, holding her hands out eagerly. Filip dug out the mermaid skins and the carved beads, and laid them out like a merchant lays out wares to a wealthy patron. The skins reeked of fish and dead seaweed, but the witch cared not for the stench. She snatched up the skins and spread them out over her hand showing off the striations and scales.

The waxy translucent skin gleamed dully in the morning light. She ran a fingernail down the length of one, listening to the soft sound it made. "Yes, these might just be perfect. Magga –"

"Here you go," the brownie said, appearing with a jeweler's loupe.

The witch took it and held it up to her eye. She peered intently through it at the skins. Magga brought a lamp closer and the witch hummed her thanks. Filip and Zaria exchanged looks over the curious behavior. Zaria shrugged.

"Does it pass muster?" asked Henrik.

The witch snapped the loupe away from her face. She held out her hand to the Stag Lord. "Our bargain is complete."

"Good," he said, clasping her hand firmly in his. "All open bargains are now complete. We should be free to pursue the next step."

She cocked an eyebrow. "Oh ho, so Master Brown proved helpful, after all."

"Very helpful," Zaria said. "We have a letter of introduction to someone he knows; someone we need to meet."

"I don't get it," Filip said, pointing to the skins. "Why did you need mermaid skins and why not just ask us directly for them?"

The witch smiled a Cheshire smile. "Come here and take a look under the magnifier."

He went over and peered at the scales. "Whoa," he exclaimed. "They're so different! They look so pretty."

"One belongs to a female mermaid and the other to a male mermaid," the witch explained.

Henrik's expression perked up; his interest piqued. "Does that signify something?"

"It does," she said. "Combined by a skillful tailor they provide the wearer protection."

"Protection from what?" Geirr asked, sitting on one of the stools.

"Fire," she said, her wrinkled face stretching wide. "Not just any fire though, but magical fire."

Aleks looked keenly at the skins laid out on the kitchen counter. "What, like from a dragon?"

She tapped a nail against the scales, flicking them back and forth with a soft *shah shah* sound. "Not a dragon, if that were the case, mermaids would be extinct, as everyone scrambles to get the skins they need for protection from those evil creatures."

"What fire?" chirruped Airi, hopping off Aleks' shoulder to the counter. She peered intently at the skins, leaning over to peck a corner.

The witch stopped her with a gentle hand to the head. "A fire from a forge," she explained. "Like those of the lower court of the dwarves in Malmdor."

Christoffer elbowed Zaria in the ribs, excitedly. "We happen to be going there next."

"Oh?" the witch said, her blue eyes brightening. "What takes you to Malmdor?"

"If you make gloves of the skins we could trade them there for you," Christoffer said, ready to help.

Henrik's pensive gaze lingered on the witch. He said softly, no accusation in his voice. "You knew we were heading there next already, didn't you?"

Her snaggletooth peeped out as she grinned wider. "Why would you come to such a conclusion, my dear Stag Lord?"

He shook his head, dropping his arms, and said dotingly, "You're too crafty for your own good."

She cackled. "I've been accused of that before."

"Aw, man," Christoffer complained, pouting. There went his bright idea. Magga sent him a superior look. He ignored her.

The Stag Lord chuckled and placed his palms on the counter. He leaned forward and said smoothly, "I suppose we should thank you for not letting us leave first before sharing the information that we need to know. I would not have relished making a third trek to your grove while eluding dragon schemes."

"Would I do that to you, Stag Lord?" she cooed.

"Yes," he said without hesitation. "Just to teach me to be more aware, so I'm alert to similar antics in future dealings with you and others."

"When you first came to me, it was like taking candy from a babe. I almost felt bad."

"No, you didn't," he teased.

"You're right, I didn't," she returned sassily.

He arched an eyebrow. "What do you wish to trade for the gloves? Nothing is free with you."

"Are you sure we need them?" asked Geirr.

Christoffer held up his hand and fake whispered, "She always knows the things we need to win."

He looked unconvinced. "What if the price is too steep to pay? She likes indentured servitude in exchange for trinkets. We don't need to do that this time."

Henrik slapped his hand on the counter. "I agree. Witch, you better not think of getting more of our time and labor. Magga will be most put out with you if you do; you'll leave her with nothing left to tend."

The witch briefly touched her hands to her chest before spreading them wide. "Who me? Never. You're my dearest friends, I give you a good deal."

The sound of seven scoffs, including Airi, startled the group and they all laughed. Even the witch laughed, but she shook her finger briskly under their noses. "Naughty, naughty, children. Do you not trust my sincerity?"

"That depends on the deal you propose for these fire-resistant mermaid gloves," Henrik said, winking at her.

"Ah, you're all grown up, aren't you? Don't be too sure you've nothing left to learn from these old bones."

"You're not bones," he said charmingly. "You're as spry and clever as ever, in fact I would say you look younger than you did."

She tittered, pleased. "Fine, fine. You win, Stag Lord. I shall name my price." The witch pulled a sealed envelope from her apron and slid it across to him. When he moved to pick it up, she stayed his hand. "Don't open it. Not yet. Inside is something you must know and must do, but only when the time is right. Do you swear to not look inside until it is clear you must do so, and do you promise to agree to my terms as described therein?"

He hesitated. "That's too broad an agreement."

The witch patted his hand. "I no longer wish for trifles like your first kiss or your child's name. Rest assured on that. What I want is more important and far-reaching. It is no little thing I am asking, nor is it something you'd be unwilling to give if you knew."

Henrik and the witch stared at each other, gazes even and open. Finally, with only the slightest hint of hesitation, he agreed to the bargain and the witch clapped her hands. A hum of magic filled the air and settled on the Elleken prince. He pocketed the envelope and Magga gathered them all up and sent them outside to wait.

The Dutch door shut firmly behind them, blocking their view of what the witch and the brownie were up to inside. They sat on the grass and enjoyed lemonade that Zaria conjured for the group. Christoffer smacked his lips, enjoying the tartness. He closed his eyes and tilted his head back, soaking up the sun.

Aleks frowned, staring into his cup and rubbing the cuff on his wrist in agitation. "Was that wise?"

Henrik shrugged, unruffled. "We had a choice to make in there. Do we trust our allies or don't we? Has she been virtuous or unscrupulous?" He spread his hands in supplication. "I'm inclined to trust her. She's not steered us wrong yet."

"You couldn't make a bargain like that with a fairy," he said, still uneasy.

"True," Henrik agreed, thinking – as Christoffer and the others were – of the many examples of greedy and power-hungry fey. "But I think you can make one like that with the witch and maybe, one day, under your rule, with a fey."

From the tree, the witch sang a tuneless off-key phrase, which she repeated with octave changing vocalizations thrown in for good measure. She sang like it was the next karaoke hit or at least like one of the female leads in his mom's dramas with lots of energy and zero embarrassment.

"Weather-wyverns be hot, my mermaid gloves be not… whoo—oo— whoo—oo— whooo—oo— whooooo… Weather-wyverns be hot, my mermaid gloves be not… whoo—oo— whoo—oo— whooo— oo—whooooo…"

Colored smoke rose from her chimney, first a deep crimson red, then a bright cheerful yellow, a puff of magenta pink, and then lavender, the last in concord grape. The smoke curled and furled like an undulating tail. As it dissipated it settled over the group and each color had a scent – fiery cherry, bright lemon, gentle rose, misty lavender, and sugared plum.

A loud bang made them all jump and look toward the front door. The witch threw the top half open and beckoned. Christoffer stood up and loped over. She held out the gloves. They were pearlescent – the off-white and waxy texture of the mermaid skins had been transformed into something smooth and supple like the inside of a shell. The gloves looked delicate and dainty and thin, very thin. He wasn't sure how they would prevent someone from getting burned. He accepted the gloves, tapping them against his forehead in thanks.

"Remember not to read what's in the envelope until the time is right."

"How will we know?" asked Filip, shading his eyes.

"You'll know," the witch promised.

They had to trust she was right.

Christoffer handed the gloves to Henrik who pocketed them with the envelope. In the end, they had their prize and the witch had hers, unknown though it was.

Chapter Eleven: The Fear Upon the Hill

Christoffer tossed a stick for Defender who sprinted for the prize. He glanced at the others picking their way through the underbrush. "What do you think is inside the envelope?"

Aleks eyed Henrik's antlered form and pursed his lips. "I'm not sure, but at this point we can only hope it's as beneficial for us as it is for the witch."

Filip swung Zaria's hand back and forth and grinned down at her. He said, "I'm on Henrik's side for this one. The witch isn't one to screw us over. She's been more fairy godmother than say, wicked witch."

"Would be bad news for us if she changed or if she'd been swayed by the dragon," Geirr said worriedly, siding with Aleks.

Zaria shook her head. "She isn't. We would know."

"Would we?" Geirr questioned. "Like how we knew Oskar had changed?"

She debated silently then said, "Yes, we'd know if she'd been swayed. We've met many individuals now who've been swayed by greed and grief, and by power and promises. We can trust our instincts here. It's unfortunate that we only found out about Oskar after reconnecting with him, but we're in close contact with the witch often enough that there shouldn't be any surprises from that quarter."

"We can't start seeing evil in good or we might as well give up now and tell the dragon we'll set it free," Henrik said. "We can trust our allies and friends."

"Sure, sure," said Christoffer, taking the stick back from Defender and throwing it again into the woods. "But what do you think is in the envelope?"

Henrik shrugged. "I couldn't even begin to guess."

Christoffer eyed him. "Do you think it's the name of your firstborn?"

Henrik paused mid step, struck by the thought, but then continued on. He said evenly, "She promised it wasn't anything she'd asked from me before."

"Well, I think it's a quest," said Christoffer. "Once we get what we need from the dwarves, I think she's going to send us somewhere dangerous to recover a lost treasure that we can only get with our soon-to-be-acquired item from Malmdor."

"O…kay," Aleks said, drawing out the syllables. "What's the item?"

"Her name," Christoffer said. "She can't be 'the witch of the woods' forever."

"You don't think she knows her own name?" Zaria asked, trying to puzzle that one out. "That seems pretty farfetched even for you."

Filip grinned. "That sounds like an adventure. What do you think her name is? You must have a theory."

"Which Witch."

"The witch of the woods," said Filip.

"Which Witch," Christoffer repeated.

Filip shook his head in confusion, and said, "The *witch*? You know, the one that wears a handkerchief on her head? Has a snaggle tooth? She lives in a tree? That witch, mate."

He nodded and smirked. "Which Witch."

"As in which witch are you talking about," Aleks explained. "This witch or that witch."

"Which Witch," Christoffer agreed giving him a thumbs up.

"Oh," said Filip shaking his head. "Sure, whatever you say, mate."

A large hill crested before them and they climbed it. Trees thinned near the top and abruptly the gentle noises of nature stopped, hushed by the atrocity before them. Defender whined and tucked into Christoffer, hugging close to his side. His tail which had been wagging moments earlier, drooped.

Christoffer couldn't believe his eyes. All across the plateau, skinny black marks blistered the ground looking like charred fingers of lightning. Dozens upon dozens of wild reindeer sprawled out over the area, mostly sitting, as if sleeping, while some lay on their sides. Their unnatural stillness told him otherwise. The wind shifted and the acrid burn at the back of his nose confirmed they'd been electrocuted.

"What's this? What happened?" asked Geirr, his blue eyes wide and uncomprehending.

Henrik hunkered down next to one and touched its flank. Feeling its cool form and sensing no movement, he glanced up at them, his features grim and harsh. "Something killed them."

"The lightning?" Zaria asked, squatting down beside him to take a closer look. With one hand she covered her face, and with the other, she reached out to close the creature's open eyes.

"There's only one dragon that I know of that wields lightning like this," Henrik said, looking sightlessly out across the sloping mountain down into the valley. "This here, –" he waved at the loss before them – "cinches it. We're dealing with—"

"Fritjof," Aleks said, looking gut-punched. "I thought I killed him. Oh God, how was I so wrong? I thought the dagger went through the eye of his storm."

"No," said Henrik firmly, cutting him off. "Fritjof is gone. He is. We saw the proof. This is Egil."

"Egil?" Aleks said, shocked. "But it's lightning. Lightning comes from a storm. Fritjof's true form was the storm."

"But just the storm, I'm thinking," said Henrik. "Just wind and rain. The lightning belonged always to Egil, like the darkness always belonged to Koll."

"Fritjof's storm definitely had lightning," Aleks countered hotly, still visibly upset, veins in his neck popping out from tension.

"It did," Zaria said, remembering.

The Stag Lord tipped his head. "I think we saw it then because Egil was starting to break free. His brother's storm was perfect cover for him to try to escape. Seeing lightning isn't unexpected in a storm, so we thought nothing of it. Didn't you say, Christoffer, that you saw something at the end of the fight?"

"I thought I did," Christoffer clarified. "Everyone said it was a trick of the light. Nobody else saw anything. A dragon is too big to hide, right?"

"The witch," said Aleks thinking hard. "I think the witch said you were right that night when I woke up after the fight. I can't remember." He rubbed his temples and looked bleakly around. "We should've listened to her sooner."

Airi flew down from his shoulder to one of the lifeless stags and perched in its antlers. She surveyed the scene and cried mournfully. "Lost friends. Friends lost."

"Egil is the dragon of fear," Zaria said reaching out to touch Aleks' sleeve. She tugged him around so he faced her. "Don't let him make you afraid. You rid the world of Fritjof. Your bravery was amazing and is not to be discounted."

"But I let one escape," he moaned, rubbing his palms over his eyes, scrubbing away grief.

She said softly, but firmly, "Egil is not your fault, just like Fritjof wasn't mine. Don't blame yourself where you wouldn't blame me."

Henrik lay a hand on the fey king's shoulder. "They are the three original brothers – they're tricky and slippery and wily and manipulative."

"Opportunistic and calculating," Geirr added. "We couldn't have predicted it and neither could you."

"We're sure it's Egil?" asked Filip.

Henrik ticked his points against his fingers. "Fearful creatures like goblins suddenly behaving differently, bolder movements by the darker groups of magical beings like hulders and hags, thousand-year-old krakens waking and rising to the surface, losing the High Court of Jötunheim as an ally due to disproportionate grief and false blame, and now this. If it isn't Egil sowing fear, some other dragon is doing a damn good job at it."

"I'm glad it wasn't the ellefolken," Zaria said, breathing out slowly, eyes sad. "I'm glad your mom kept them on the move."

"Me, too," he said. "We need to tell everyone."

They all agreed and moved away, leaving the horrible scene behind them. Aleks sent Airi off with a message to deliver to his girlfriend and another to his sister. Gjallarhorns rang out in pleasant little tunes as he and Henrik took turns calling and talking to Olebjørn, Queen Silje, King Flein, Queen Wenche, and King Kafirr.

Aleks found Olebjørn in Rjupa the Measureless' court. They'd been in the middle of a meeting with the giantess and having some success. The news of Egil and the latest attack only strengthened their position among her court. Aleks rang off feeling good about their chances of convincing the giantess to not only help in the pending showdown but to get the remaining tribes on board as well.

Queen Silje's reaction to the news about the dragon was to inform Henrik about her findings with the goblins. One had returned and tried to eat the flesh of his dead fellows. Her elven guard captured the pitiful creature and attempted to interrogate it, but he lacked the verbal skills or the understanding and so was dispatched. She and the Stag Lord agreed to a coordinated effort to double down on the patrols near the Gjallarbrú and surrounding Gloomwood Forest.

Feeling less enthusiastic to contact King Flein, Aleks nevertheless reached out. The dwarf king immediately called up his guards and commanded them to check on his son in the prison to ensure there was nothing suspicious there. He ruefully told Aleks that the trial for Prince Floki was still in progress and that his son, despite repeated attempts to talk sense into him, was still unrepentant. Aleks grimaced at the news and hung up, not satisfied with the interaction.

"I'm surprised it's still dragging out," Geirr said.

"The royal family is entitled to the best defense council available," Henrik said. "The defense gets first pick from the royal retainers."

"Isn't that just a load of dung," Christoffer said.

"If Floki wins his freedom, you know he's going straight to Egil," Filip said.

He smirked. "If I was Egil, I would refuse him as a henchman, he's been incompetent twice."

"What's the news from your mother?" Aleks asked Henrik. "Is Elleken safe?"

Henrik slung his bag to his other shoulder and nodded once. "They're safe. She's kept them moving. There's been grumblings because the camp isn't meant to move but a few times a year and they're packing and moving every few days. She's going to send more ellefolken to Queen Silje to help with the elves' patrols. She wasn't happy to lose them, but saw why it was prudent to provide support."

"Last, but not least, King Kafirr," Aleks said and called the troll king.

The gjallarhorn rang in a triumphant peal for a few moments until Captain Morvin appeared in view. Aleks' eyes widened in surprise, but he greeted the head of the Black-Tailed Ribcage Butcher family with equanimity. "You were not the one I was expecting on this line. How are you?"

"King Aleks how nice to see you," the mountain-troll said, which Christoffer supposed to be true as it was Aleks and the rest of the gang who'd rescued the Firstborn of the great houses, which included Captain Morvin's daughter Kanutte. The mountain-troll was bound to feel some affection for them. "To what pleasure do we owe this call?"

"Pleasure, not so much," Aleks said. "I'm alerting your king to new developments which he should be aware of in the region."

"Is this about Olebjørn? We are greatly concerned about river-trolls consolidating their power and becoming multi-headed."

"Is that because their power now outstrips King Kafirr's?" Christoffer asked, leaning into the frame.

Captain Morvin didn't twitch or betray anything with his expression, which kind of sealed it for Christoffer. He knew this had to be a sore spot for King Kafirr, because his power and throne had only recently been reclaimed after eliminating Jorkden, the leader of the Wild Hunt. Having a new troll on the scene whose power could cast the mountain-troll's power and abilities into doubt was not ideal.

Henrik leaned into the frame from the other side. Looking squarely at Morvin, he said, "This is not about the river-troll. This is about the dragon on the loose that caused them to team up in the first place."

Morvin canted his head, his interest piqued. "Which dragon?"

"Egil we believe due to several recent events."

"Do tell," Morvin invited and so they did, filling in the troll captain with all the details. At the end, he said, "I had heard of course, from my future son-in-law, several of these events, but this new one with the reindeer is the dented club."

"Is that anything like the phrase, 'a smoking gun?'" Christoffer asked.

"When's the wedding?" Aleks asked, steering it away from his segue before Morvin commented on the trollish idiom.

"After they've hunted together ninety-nine times. Their one hundredth will be part of their wedding ceremony."

"What are they at now?" Geirr asked.

He was probably thinking that with Kanutte's bloodthirsty personality and Falkor's impressive bulk and leadership among the firstborn, the young mountain-trolls had to be near their ninety-ninth hunt.

"I've only just granted them permission to hunt together," said Morvin. "Tonight will be their third hunt together. I will tell them to look for goblins."

"Falkor and his friends were doing that when we met."

"That was a patrol, which is altogether different, and not the same," Morvin said.

"What's the difference?" asked Filip.

"Isn't it obvious?" Christoffer asked, slyly. "It's a classic case of cold pursuit versus hot pursuit."

"You're not wrong," Morvin deadpanned. "I must go now. I will inform my king of your suspicions."

Henrik held up a hand. "Before you go, I humbly request that you ask King Kafirr to reach out to Queen Silje or my mother. With Trolgar's aid patrolling the region of Gloomwood Forest our safety is guaranteed and nobody will be spread thin. It's imperative we're not surprised by another attack from Egil's faction."

Morvin's mustache twitched in agitation as he looked over his shoulder at something they couldn't see. He said abstractedly, "I will pass along your petition, but I make no promises."

"Fair enough," Aleks said and hung up the call. Morvin's holographic appearance winked out of existence and he put away his gjallarhorn.

Henrik remained stoic and silent, which instantly caught Christoffer's attention. "What's wrong?" he asked as they began their northerly journey once more.

"I hope we did the right thing," he said pensively. "You all remember how King Kafirr's allegiance flip-flopped during the Dragomir Wars?"

"I mean we weren't there, but sure, I think we've heard something to that effect from Zaria once," he said.

The Stag Lord gave him a look. "You know what I mean. The dragon that swayed the mountain-troll king to betray us was –"

"Don't say it," warned Geirr, groaning in anticipation.

"Egil," Henrik finished.

"He said it," said Christoffer cheekily.

Geirr groaned again. "Peachy, just peachy."

Zaria frowned unhappily. "It was the Seiland giants who told us Kaffir and his father swapped sides three times before the war ended."

"It's common history," the Stag Lord said. "They were in the alliance with everyone against the dragons, but then they fell into Egil's clutches."

"What happened?" Zaria asked.

He swept the antlered hood back and ran his hand through his hair. "Something caused King Kafirr to switch back. He never revealed what it was that turned him – either against or for us. My father and grandfather felt it was something private so they never pried, but rumors are he lost his firstborn."

Christoffer raised his hand. "How can that be a rumor? Wouldn't someone know? Someone other than the king, I mean? Where *is* his firstborn?"

"Allegedly, his firstborn hasn't been born," he said.

"Allegedly?" Aleks pressed. "Wouldn't a king's child and heir be announced to all the realms?"

"It would," the Stag Lord agreed. "If the child was born while Trolgar had been allied with us. Otherwise, a newborn babe, even a troll, is a vulnerability during wartimes, and if we were considered Trolgar's enemies I don't think we would've known."

"But of course, that wouldn't have been condoned by our side," Zaria stated. "Exploiting a child for the sake of the war. I can't picture Queen Helena allowing that under her watch."

"There were those who might've tried," Henrik said.

"The fey," Aleks guessed. "I can see my father advocating for the firstborn to be captured or killed."

Henrik rubbed his chin and said, "It's a moot point in any case as the child's existence has never been confirmed. We must take the lack of firstborn at face value until told otherwise."

Zaria shuddered and held her arms. "I don't like it, and I don't like the fact that it is Oskar who appears to be flip-flopping now."

Christoffer tossed her a smirk, "Instead of Oskar the Elevated he should be known as Oskar the Vacillating, or maybe the Vast-ill-king."

They all groaned at that.

The trees thinned out and the ground grew rockier. Spread out before them, the abandoned quarry hiding the entrance to Malmdor was all cut surfaces and glassy sunlit pools. The lake had dried up in many spots that, before, had been shallow. Drought or something else, maybe even the lack of a certain water-wyvern, must've caused it to evaporate. The remaining water, undisturbed by wind due to the rocky walls surrounding it, reflected the sky so perfectly that it seemed down was up and up was down, a dizzying effect from so high.

"No water-wyverns down there today," Christoffer said. "Unless they're the size of guppies."

"I kind of miss that cheeky little booger," Filip said, looking down over the lip of the quarry.

"He was immensely helpful in Niffleheim," Aleks agreed and Christoffer was reminded that he'd missed out on that because he'd been the last one found during his friend's trials in the Autumn Court. Being a sidekick was tough and sometimes unrelentingly boring when one wasn't part of the main action.

"Less so in Malmdor, though," Geirr pointed out.

"Zaaaria," Christoffer singsonged. "I don't want to trip along dangerous, barely there, and partially caved-in footpaths. Would you pleeeease teleport me to the bottom?"

She laughed. "I guess it's better than dodging a hungry water-wyvern." He whooped, and she added, "but not by much."

"Ah, man, wound me some more," he whined. "It's okay, I can take it. Nobody loves me."

"I certainly do love you, silly goose, which is why I'm sparing you the trip down."

She grabbed hold of him and Filip and concentrated for a moment. The air constricted slightly and static electricity buzzed along his skin. With a shimmer and a humming sigh, they reappeared down below. The static discharged in a burst before building up again as she transitioned between their location and the top of the quarry.

Back and forth she went until they were all brought down, including Defender who was not happy about it. He whined unhappily and tucked himself behind Christoffer's legs. Laying a hand on him, he said softly, "Whoa, boy. It's all right. You're okay. No more nasty magic trips for you. I promise."

Henrik took out the device his father, Hector, had used once before and stood next to the biggest pool of water in the quarry bed. He blew a single note into it and a gentle, unforgettable, tune echoed around the quarry. The musical notes rippled the water like wind stirring the tides. From the center of the pool a rowboat surfaced from the unseen depths below and glided across the waves to the shore where they stood.

The dilapidated boat smelled like rotten seaweed and had peeling paint and warped boards. Aleks appeared as unimpressed by it as he'd been before, but Christoffer eagerly climbed in, ready to be sucked down into the whirlpool at the pool's center and into the abandoned, flooded palace of Malmdor. Looking back at the others, he saw that Geirr was a little green around the gills again, as he, too, remembered the upcoming whirlpool with its fast-spinning cyclone.

"You going to barf?" he asked.

"If I do, I'll aim for you," Geirr said spitefully.

"I got a plan for it," Zaria told him, laying a reassuring hand on his arm.

When they were all seated the boat began gliding toward the center of the quarry. Ahead, the whirlpool spun and the sound of rushing water picked up to a dull roar. Geirr clutched the edges of the boat and hung on for dear life as they began spinning. The boat sunk lower into the heart of the whirlpool, but before it got worse Zaria's magic encircled the boat and lifted it up and into the empty center.

She lowered them through the opening and into the cavern below, letting it land gently, avoiding the splash of the whirlpool's waterfalls. The boat bobbed unsteadily and settled, the bottom hitting the hard ground under the waters. Christoffer winced and rubbed his tailbone. They had arrived.

Chapter Twelve: Ghouls Make for Terrible Pets

Water dripped steadily down in little rivulets here and there where the seal above wasn't tight. Standing in ankle-deep water, Christoffer spun around to get a good look at their surroundings. The water level was lower than he remembered from the last time they were here, roughly three years ago. It would make traveling through the passages easier. No swimming required.

"I never asked last time, but what happens to the boat?" Christoffer asked, nudging the side with his foot which caused it to bob drunkenly for a moment.

Henrik put away the musical instrument he held, slipping it into his bag, taking a moment to shrug into it. "I think it stays here until it's called up to the surface."

"I sink you're right," he said.

"Canoe think of any worse puns?" Geirr drawled, laughing.

"Come on yawl, you know you can't beat me in a pun-off. I live for this," he joked.

Geirr's eyes lit with the challenge. "Well frigate, I bow to your wisdom then."

He puffed out his chest, "I do possess an in-oar-dinate amount of sail-ient advice."

Aleks appeared between them, grinning. "That was a yacht of good puns, now let's focus on what we're here to do and not go overboard."

"Sure, spoil our fun for the hull of it," Christoffer pouted, but pivoted and refocused on the dimly lit cavern.

The pear-shaped room shimmered from glowing purple mineral in the walls. The room branched off into three tunnels disappearing into the dark. Faint patterns of the purple mineral, clearly dwarf-laid, denoted each path like a coded message. These patterns, which before had been hidden under the water, could be useful for navigation.

Aleks examined them before pointing at the middle passage. "We want to go this way," he said.

Henrik pointed right, "That way is warmer, isn't it? The forges should be this way."

"I remember going left takes us toward the palace," Zaria said, repinning her braid in place and smoothing down the flyaways.

"So not that way," Geirr said drily.

"Agreed. No mermaids for me again any time soon," Christoffer said remembering stumbling upon one in the flooded passages.

"You're one to talk," Filip said, laughing and shuddering exaggeratedly at the same time. "If I never see another one again, I'm a happy man."

"We don't want to go right," Aleks said, interrupting. "My fey gift is saying the middle passage is the one we want to take."

"That's good enough for me," Christoffer said and began to slog his way over to it.

"All right," Henrik said, falling into step with him, splashing through the water. "There must be some hidden merit in choosing this path."

Zaria smiled back at them. "I think so, too. Aleks is never wrong about this stuff. Imagine how much harder our fight with Fritjof would've been without Zorka. If we hadn't stumbled into King Kaffir in the dungeons, we would never have met her."

They traveled through the tunnel two by two. The path forward sloped and turned and branched off again, and again, and again. Following Aleks' directions, they forged their way ahead, zig-zagging through the maze of tunnels.

The further into the mountain they went, the more the water receded. When the water petered out, Christoffer and the others dripped all over dry ground, leaving behind phantom footprints that evaporated in the drafty tunnel.

Squelching noises echoed and magnified in the empty space until Zaria couldn't stand it and forced them all to stop and remove their shoes. She blasted their shoes, and them, with hot air to eliminate the damp. Christoffer groaned in pleasure as his chilled toes sunk into the hot interior of his shoes.

"It's like they've been in the dryer," Filip said, wiggling his toes in his shoes. "Thanks, Zar-Zar!"

"Much better," she said as they began walking again and the squeakiness didn't return.

The hairs on Christoffer's arms rose in warning. The back of his neck prickled. His mouth dried. Licking his suddenly parched lips, he whisper-shouted, "Hey, Aleks, I think we should stop."

He and Geirr turned the corner ahead of them, too busy talking and missed the warning. But Zaria and Filip heard and paused, looking back at him and Henrik. Everyone looked at him curiously, but he wasn't sure what to say. "Something's not right," he managed to explain just before a shout and a shriek ricocheted off the stone walls.

As one, they spun back toward the corner and sprinted to it. Rounding it, Christoffer had to reign in a shriek himself. He clutched the back of Zaria's sweater as terror gripped him and his eyes struggled to comprehend what he saw.

The purple glow from the ore in the walls stopped, barely penetrating the darkened hall. Someone had intentionally dug out the inlaid patterns. Ghostly, gray shadows tracked them with bulbous milky colored-eyes. A faint rattling sound, *clinked, clinked, clinked*.

He scanned the darkness for Aleks and Geirr and found them a little further in. Aleks clung to Geirr's arms, pulling with all his might. One of the hideous creatures clung to Geirr's shoeless foot with ash gray claws, pulling with equal strength. Its gaping mouth revealed needle-thin teeth dripping with black saliva.

"I'm going to reach for a coin," Aleks said quietly, soothingly trying not to draw attention.

"Don't let go," Geirr shouted, alarmed.

Aleks' eyes widened. "Okay. Okay, I won't."

Zaria tossed a purple fireball down the corridor, scaring the creature and others like it.

"No light," it hissed, letting Geirr go.

The creature cowered in the slim shadows. From its raised arms flashed metal handcuffs and a length of chain anchoring it to the wall behind.

"What is that thing?" Geirr asked, scrambling back as fast as he could, sacrificing his shoe to his attacker.

"That is a ghoul," Henrik said, leaning over to help him stand. "You're lucky to be alive. If that thing had bit you —" he trailed off, grimacing.

Geirr stared, horrified, down the length of the tunnel. "They're all ghouls."

"They're all chained," Zaria said, moving her fireball down the hall.

The ghouls cringed away from her magical light, averting their gazes. They swayed back and forth as if in a trance, their gaunt faces taut with hunger. Metal clinked against metal as they shifted and writhed.

Geirr's complexion still hadn't recovered, his pallid skin nearly as ashen as the ghouls'.

"Who keeps ghouls as pets?" Christoffer asked.

Aleks shook his head, the coin he wanted earlier now in his hand. He moved it nervously through his fingers. "I don't know, but I don't think we should find out."

"Are you saying we backtrack?" asked Henrik.

The fey king hesitated. "No. My mental map is telling me we should press on down this tunnel."

"Past the ghouls?" Geirr asked, incredulous. "No way. No damn way. Not the slightest chance. I nearly died."

"You didn't nearly die," Zaria corrected gently. "You're alive and well. You weren't bitten. That didn't happen. You're safe. You're well."

"Right," said Filip. "Nothing happened."

"And I'd like to keep it that way," he retorted, color returning to his face. He let out a pent-up breath and dusted off his pants. "I suppose you're right, though. I wasn't bitten, I am safe, I didn't die."

"And we'd like to keep it that way," she said, a faint smile about her lips.

"I was just about to say that," Christoffer complained causing them all to laugh.

"So now what?" asked Filip, looking at Aleks. "Is there a way around perhaps?"

Aleks closed his eyes to concentrate. After a moment he opened them and shook his head. "I was right the first time. There's only through."

"What's on the other side?" asked Geirr warily.

He ran a hand through his red hair and gestured beyond the glow of Zaria's fireball. "I believe it's Aumak. I think she lives down there."

"She's not very welcoming to visitors," Christoffer noted, toeing a rock with his shoe.

"No, she is not," agreed Geirr, before asking the most important question pressing on all their minds. "How do we get past the ghouls?"

"Zaria's magic," said Henrik. "It's the only way. They don't appear to like the light."

"I don't particularly like them under this purple light either," Geirr said. "They look ghastly."

"One could say ghoulish," Christoffer quipped. Geirr shot him a dirty look, while Zaria choked on a giggle.

"Stick to the center of the hall," warned Henrik, nodding to Zaria to toss another fireball.

She did, and the shadows grew slimmer, the glowing orbs following in front and behind as protection against the ghouls' hungry gazes. As they approached, the nightmarish creatures hissed, shrinking back against the walls. Their pitiful cries tugged at Christoffer and he had to remind himself these things were so lost to sense that they fed on the corpses of their own kind. Yuck.

He stared at them hard as they passed by, single file, shuffling down the center column of stone pavers, away from the walls. Flesh peeled and bubbled, teeth gnashed, and slimy wet tongues snuck between thin scaly lips. He caught one or two glaring back, deep wells of irrational anger spilling out. He rubbed his arms, trying to rid his skin of the feel of their gaze. The angrier of them lunged against their chains, ash-gray fingers stretching out, yellow nails desperate to snatch their clothes and limbs.

"Man flesh taste good," one hissed.

"Taste good, taste good, taste good," the others chanted, gaining courage. They threw themselves against their chains, rattling them, laughing when the friends shrank back into the grasping hands of their fellows.

One of them scratched at him, fingers sliding briefly through his hair. He fought the urge to bat the hand away, not daring to give it a better target. He could afford to lose some hair, but not his hand or his life. The others must be experiencing the same thing as they huddled closer together, taking mincing steps forward.

Christoffer closed his eyes and held onto the back of Filip's denim jacket. He prayed through every step down that hallway, listening to the clinking metal and garbled hissing words. He would not fear evil. He would not. No matter how scary it hissed at him. He heard Geirr whispering behind him, offering up his own prayers.

"We made it through," Aleks announced, a second before Christoffer slammed into Filip's back nearly toppling them over.

"Steady now," Henrik said, righting them.

"I feel like we just walked past starving lions," Geirr said, tugging his coat together and stuffing his hands inside. He trembled a little. "Why do we keep facing one harrowing trial after another? I'm going to have nightmares for life. Literally, I will be sleeping, and my brain will take me right back here, in the dark, without you all beside me, and they will eat me."

"Well, not literally, literally," Christoffer said. "You can't die in your nightmares."

"You say that now, but I bet mares live for this kind of fertile horror-filled mindscape."

A pair of ruby red lips sprung to his mind.

He batted them away like they were gnats flying around by his head. He opened his mouth to say something, but the Stag Lord beat him to it.

"If it's of any help, I'm sure this isn't the worst thing we'll face," Henrik said.

Geirr gave him a look filled with deepest loathing. "I repeat myself, why is it we have to be the ones to face down these horrors? Why isn't it a giant tree-eating rabbit? Why must it be a kraken? Why not a fire burping lizard? Why is it the dragon of fear?"

Christoffer looked absently behind them at the tunnel they'd just walked through, feeling his heart rate slow. He murmured, softly, "Because we must go through the crucible and come out changed on the other side."

"That, and they make for a better perimeter alarm than just about anything else on earth," a husky, amused voice said.

Christoffer whipped around to see a female dwarf wearing a gray tunic in the same shade as the ghouls' skin tone. No wonder they hadn't spotted her earlier. She blended in. Her hair was also gray, and if it wasn't for her amber skin and eyes he'd have pegged her as a ghoul herself, in the same way that owners begin to look like their pets.

She watched them curiously, arms crossed. He scanned for her missing hand but it was tucked away. She caught him at it and raised an eyebrow. He flushed, mortified and glanced away.

"Aumak?" ventured Henrik.

"Aye," she answered, warily. "What are you children doing here?"

"We come to you for help," he said, reaching into his breast pocket. "Master Brown provided a letter of introduction."

She uncrossed her arms, and held out a hand to take the note. The other one, tucked by her side, Christoffer observed, was covered in a black glove with silver stitching. Aumak scanned the missive and snorted. "This isn't a letter from Master Brown. What are you all playing at?"

"My apologies. That was the wrong one." Embarrassed, Henrik snatched it back and handed her another similar sized envelope.

She took this one and nimbly plucked it from the envelope singlehanded. She read the new letter even faster. With a look of contempt, she crumped the letter and tossed it on the floor. "That old shoe leather. I can't believe he'd ask me to introduce you to the Master Gyllenhammar. As if I would spend any time with that old bat."

"Oh please," Zaria said urgently. "I know there must be a lot of history between you two as she's your grandmother –"

Aumak gasped. "That creaky little badger told you about that? What else did he say? Did he tell you why I lost my hand? I saw this one looking at it earlier." She waved the offending limb in his direction and Christoffer inwardly cringed.

"Sorry, sorry, I wasn't trying to be nosy."

"I won't do it," Aumak said firmly and at her raised voice the ghouls behind them in the tunnel began whispering and scratching at the walls.

"You must," said Zaria. "It's urgent. Egil is a threat and we need the weapons to face him."

"Can we please take this conversation somewhere else?" Geirr begged as the ghouls grew louder, moaning in hunger.

Aumak eyed the shaken young man and then the anxious sorceress before grudgingly opening the door she guarded. "I don't like visitors. Do not get comfortable; you won't be staying long."

"Thank you," Geirr said fervently, slipping inside as fast as he could.

When the door shut, the clinking chains and groaning voices of the ghouls outside turned off like a faucet.

The soundproofing was seriously top notch. The place was almost peaceful if one could ignore the constant raising of the hair on one's nape.

Aumak's home was a junkyard of delights. Tools and scraps of metal littered every surface of Aumak's cut-rock home. Debris piled so high it threatened to topple over any moment. Christoffer poked through things without permission, drawn to the twisted pieces of metal. He noticed what appeared to be an artistic sculpture hiding under a tablecloth in the corner.

"You do realize that keeping ghouls in these troubled times is a risky endeavor, right?" Henrik asked, breaking the pregnant silence. "Ghouls and goblins are not behaving in the expected manner."

"So you say, but I find them excellent deterrents from troublesome people."

"There was an attack on the elves' post at the Gjallarbrú," he pressed. "They ate the guards."

"I'm a dwarf, not an elf. I'm far superior in intelligence. Besides, I have them tied up in such a way as to not get in the way of their teeth. I'll be fine."

"But what if –"

"What did you mean by weapons?" Aumak asked bluntly changing the subject.

Zaria looked to Aleks, but whatever silent communion the two normally had going on seemed to short-circuit amongst all that metal. She said, "We need a sword like the Drakeland Sword."

Aleks thew his hands up in exasperation. "It's supposed to be a secret mission."

She stared at him. "We're going to need the dwarves and it sounds like we need the Master Gyllenhammar most of all. Being honest with her granddaughter seems like a good place to start."

Mostly honest anyway. No sense in letting go the fact that it wasn't that they needed swords *like* the Drakeland Sword, they needed the *real* Drakeland Sword fixed. If the princess of the Under Realm felt the least bit compelled to share that fact before services were secured, Christoffer was sure Aleks would tackle her to the ground.

"My grandmother will charge you a hefty sum," Aumak warned. "Can you afford her price?"

"The Under Realm can pay," she said.

Could it? Christoffer never asked, but he assumed his friend was quite rich since she was a princess. Somehow, though, he didn't think Aumak meant in gold and jewels, the typical currency of the dwarves. Her grandmother must want something else.

Aumak grunted. "If she doesn't make them herself, you would be wise to test the quality. Nobody in the guilds has made a weapon like the Drakeland Sword since the Dragomir Wars and subsequent treaty."

"The Under Realm is prepared to pay for quality, not quantity. My mother wishes me to have a matched sword so I can fight alongside her."

"Do you have the Drakeland Sword on you now?" asked Aumak, looking interestedly at her waist.

Zaria shook her head and lied her pretty head off. "Mother is using it in the Under Realm. She's trying to contain Egil, to keep him from escaping."

It was an Oscar-worthy performance, but was it enough to convince the dwarf woman before them? The room seemed to be holding its collective breath, which meant a distraction was needed. He opened his mouth and said the first thing that came to mind, "How did you lose your hand?"

He could practically feel his friends groaning in despair behind him, but he ignored them. He was on a self-imposed mission to distract Aumak, to pull her thoughts away from the Drakeland Sword, and he would not be swayed.

Aumak's gaze narrowed. "Did not Master Brown tell you all about it?"

He shrugged nonchalantly. "Vaguely. He's been getting gossipy in his old age, but he didn't spill the beans about this, just sort of hinted at it."

"It's gruesome," she said, and when none of them demurred, she sighed in capitulation. "I was going for my Platinum Guild Certification. It's the lowest level requirement to qualify for my grandmother's guild. The Gyllenhammar Flame is a coveted guild which has the prestige of producing the Drakeland Sword. If you join that guild, you are one of the best smiths in your field. Armorers, bladesmiths, metalsmiths, machinists, locksmiths, and jewelers all aim to join by any means necessary.

"It happened in the middle of my certification exam. One of the judges, a guildmaster from a lower guild, sabotaged the forge. Three weather-wyverns were employed in that forge, one for each smith in the examination. A good weather-wyvern is worth its weight a hundred times over in its ability to labor and heat a forge, and if that weren't enough of a reason to cherish one of these creatures, they're as loyal as any winter-wyvern and just as sweet."

Christoffer found that hard to believe. He recalled the broken statue covered in spikes that they'd found in Malmdor on their last visit. That scaly thing didn't seem snuggly or sweet.

"The first forge cracked and caved-in on one of the weather-wyverns, killing it instantly. Its shriek of pain short-lived. The smith was beside herself and I couldn't blame her. She lost her livelihood and certification in one fell swoop. The smith on my other side was a smug bastard – he blamed the dwarf for her loss as did the judges and my grandmother. There's no softness in her, no doubt a byproduct of being the head smith maybe. You don't get that position without being as hard as the steel you quench.

"I, too, blamed the smith, until I noticed a repeat of the same treachery on my forge. A hairline fissure split the outer wall where somebody had thinned it out on purpose. I had just moments to decide. Lose my weather-wyvern and sacrifice my reputation, or risk it all on rescuing the beasty to try to certify another day. I wasn't going to pass the examination, not if the forge fell, so it'd all come down to this one decision.

"I'd hand-raised my baby, so there was no question what I'd do. I plunged my hand into the fiery furnace and yanked him out. The forge collapsed, trapping my hand inside the blaze. My precious baby though was safe. My grandmother was not happy with my choice, as I'd lost all use of my hand. She banished me from the guilds, including the ones I'd earned membership in, and blackballed me.

"Why? To teach me a lesson, I suppose. That a bladesmith's hands – not their weather-wyvern – are their livelihood."

She paused there to examine her gloved hand. Toenails clicked on the stone, drawing the dwarf's attention.

"There he is now," Aumak said, leaning forward. "The weather-wyvern I gave my hand to save. Let me introduce him. Come here my little goober. Come say hello." To them she said, "Have you ever seen one in person before? If not, you're in for a real treat."

Chapter Thirteen: My Good Friend "Hank"

Defender growled at the weather-wyvern, hackles raised. Christoffer's tight grip was the only thing keeping the border collie from lunging and snapping. The beast hissed like an angry Komodo dragon, its throat reddening like a boiler with the start of flames. Heat radiated from where it stood, protecting an outwardly calm Aumak.

With a short command from the dwarf, the weather-wyvern dropped its stance and leapt clumsily onto the couch. While she scratched it behind its horns, he hushed his dog and got him to stand down. The weather-wyvern smugly watched from his position. Defender glared back, but behaved, sticking close to him. Christoffer petted him, smoothing down his fur.

"It's all right, boy," he soothed. "Stay next to me."

Together they watched the beast. The weather-wyvern, like all wyverns, was an amalgamation of different animals. Its head and body were lizard, while its feet were bird, and its tail resembled a lion's. On its head grew two, large, gently curving horns very much like a goat's. Unlike a winter-wyvern the size of a bear, or a water-wyvern the size of a bus, weather-wyverns were small. Both dog and weather-wyvern were equally sized, but with different body builds.

"Meet Hank," Aumak said, bussing the beast on the nose. "He's the smartest, cleverest, little goober."

"May I touch him?" Zaria asked, stretching forth a hand to touch his crown. Hank hissed, whipping his tail back and forth agitatedly and she hastily withdrew. "Perhaps some other time."

Aleks patted her shoulder consolingly. "Don't take any heed. Hank is protecting his master. Airi behaves similarly around strangers with me in Niffleheim."

Christoffer offered a slight smile. "Defender is also the same. He's only just managing to stay alert and obedient to me. He wants to challenge Hank."

"Hank wants to challenge him," Aumak said, chuckling and stroking his back between the spikes. "He's posturing and acting up, trying to incite your dog. He's hopeful for some action. Alas, I keep him too cooped up."

"The ghouls not enough challenge for him?" Geirr asked, drily.

"Their bite is too dangerous," she said. "They are not allowed to interact."

"I noticed bits of metalwork you have in here," Zaria said, looking around. "Are they all yours?"

Aumak inclined her head, gray hair slipping out from the leather thong she'd used to tie it back. "I practice to keep up my skills. Not that anything is close to the caliber I used to put out."

"I don't know," Zaria said, tilting her head and indicating the cloth-covered object. "I bet that one is pretty special. Why do you have it covered?"

"It's not finished," Aumak said. "That's the piece I was building during the certification. It's a reminder."

"What is it?" asked Aleks, leaning forward, trying to sneak a peek underneath.

She heaved herself off the couch and ambled over. With a flourish, she flicked away the cloth and revealed, "A sword."

"Wow," said Christoffer, gaping at the weapon. "That's unfinished?"

She snorted. "Of course it is, can't you see how unrefined it is? It's not even quenched, let alone sharpened, acid-etched, or outfitted with handle."

"But look at the shape," he said. "It looks like you cut it with a laser. Your lines are so clean. Are you sure you forged this?"

She crossed her arms and smirked. "Behold the talent of dwarves."

"Masterful," he said. "If this was the quality of your work, it's no wonder you're pissed about what happened."

She straightened up and shook her arm, revealing the gloved hand. "Even with this, I won't be slowed down. I'll regain all my finesse again. Every day is better than before and I have Hank. He's worth a hand or two."

"I feel that way about Defender," Christoffer said. "Though I'm still sorry you lost yours."

"Me too, kid," she said. Aumak squared her shoulders and seemed to make a decision. "Come along, I will introduce you to grandmother."

"Thank you," Zaria said, standing and gathering her bag. She clutched it tight. "You don't know how much this means to me and my mother."

266

"I reckon I might," Aumak said, eyeing the bag. "Come. Follow me."

They followed her back to her front door. Aumak removed a torch from a wall sconce and tugged on the metal arm. It decompressed with a soft hiss. Silence held for a moment before a grinding noise echoed around them. Christoffer looked for the source but couldn't see anything.

"What's happening?" asked Geirr.

Aumak opened her front door. "The ghouls have been safely removed from the corridor."

"Oh good," Filip said. "I wasn't looking forward to making my way back through them. The touch of their fingers makes my skin crawl."

"Mine too," Geirr said, rubbing his arms. "Were they for us, or do you torture all your visitors that way?"

"Only the unwelcomed and unannounced ones," she said mildly.

"Great," Christoffer enthused. "So that means no more ghouls for us as we're friends now."

"I wouldn't go so far as to say that," she said, chuckling despite herself.

Aumak placed the torch in the empty sconce at the end of the tunnel, which felt much shorter now that one didn't have to bypass ghouls to traverse it. The weight of the torch triggered the mechanism and the walls began shifting. Stone slid from side to side as secret compartments were revealed and the ghouls reemerged. They groaned and moaned and snarled and sniffed the air.

"Hungry," the nearest one hissed, spittle dripping from its lips.

"You'll have your meat," Aumak said. "I will be back with it. Now, guard."

"You trained them?" Henrik asked, astounded.

"Ghouls can be managed," she said matter-of-factly.

Christoffer caught sight of several pairs of glowing, malicious eyes. He shook his head, "I think one is overkill, but thirteen? Did you need to have a whole shroud of them? What can thirteen do that one can't?"

She snorted. "A shroud of ghouls, a malignity of goblins, a grievance of visitors, a shortage of wits."

He laughed. "A shortage of wits; I'll need to remember that one."

"I think she meant for you to remember the grievance of visitors," Geirr commented.

Filip laughed. "Him or Master Brown."

"Hmm," Aumak hummed. "Yes, Master Brown will be hearing from me after all this. He better watch his collection of teapots."

As they moved to leave, the ghouls shifted and crouched, eyeing Christoffer and the others. His skin crawled in warning as a baker's dozen pairs of eyes tracked their movements. Hastily, he slipped around the corner, dragging Defender with him, moving swiftly back toward the main branches in the tunnels.

With Aumak as their guide, Aleks got a reprieve. She efficiently cut a path through the maze of tunnels and offshoots. Noises began to reach them, the steady background hum of a bustling city. Soon the hum turned into murmurings, where the occasional shout broke through.

"You call this diamond quality? At best it's bronze. I won't pay more than two rubies for it."

"Swindler, my unborn son could forge better than this hunk of junk!"

"You're a waste of coal, Smithers, get out of my way. I'll deal with the customers. You go restock the forge in the back."

"Harsh crowd," Aleks whispered.

Aumuk heard and bared her teeth. "When most of us can make what we want, why accept poor quality goods?"

"What about magical items?" Henrik asked, casting his gaze around the teeming market place.

"Magic is a luxury few can afford," she said with a shrug. "Quality goods with magic infused in them can ask for their own price."

"But you have all those magic mirrors," Zaria said, her brow knitting. "Don't you have magic wielders?"

"Those are made from the ore in these mountains. It's already infused with magic. You've seen it glow from how much is present even in small quantities."

"But how is the intent shaped?" she pressed. "Because the mirrors are different than the Drakeland Sword and yet come from the same ore."

"The only ones who knew, are gone," Aumak said. "I told you, your quest to get another dragon-defying weapon is pointless."

"Pun intended?" Christoffer asked Filip.

"Only if it were *toothless* too," he countered.

"Who will bid on this scrawny lad?" a voice shouted over the crowd.

Geirr halted in his tracks and spun around looking for the voice. Christoffer too, and they found the auctioneer standing in the center of a stage, prodding a young dwarf lad forward. The boy was wearing chains and appeared to be half-starved.

"This is too barbaric," Zaria hissed, purple magic gathering on her fingers.

"I can't believe you have slave trading," Geirr said, disgusted.

"I thought it was an empty threat by Olaf," Christoffer said, paling at the thought of the horrific fate that might have been his.

"It's an ugly practice," Aumak agreed. "But it's not exactly slave trading. This is the Apprentice Market. That kid has been offered up by his parents who are in debt.

"He'll enter an apprentice contract and learn a trade provided he possesses any skill. He'll be with and help his Master until he pays back his education and his parent's debts."

"How is that better?" Zaria asked, shaking her head, her purple eyes large in her head.

"Keep moving," Aumak said. "Don't draw attention."

"No," Filip said, grabbing Zaria's sparking hand. "Not until we understand."

She shrugged and crossed her arms. "Usually, parents have to buy an apprenticeship for their children. Here they're being paid to offer an apprentice."

Aleks crossed his arms and gritted his teeth. "Indentured servitude, really? That's hardly better. What safeguards are in place? How is the child's safety guaranteed? What about fair and equitable treatment? Where is the law on setting contractual terms and working limits?"

"There are no guarantees, that's why I said it was an ugly practice. Tis far better to learn when you are not indebted to your Master. Sought after Masters never seek a child from these markets."

"Never?" Filip said. "Even when they could benefit that child more than any other? Selfish."

"Or kind; if the other apprentices knew you were essentially a charity case it would be open season. When you're a thrall you don't want that kind of attention. Your rights are nonexistent. You belong to your Master."

"So basically, thralls are the same as runts," Zaria said, jaw tight.

"I know what I'm asking from King Flein," Aleks said darkly as the auction closed and the child was purchased for six rubies, four sapphires, and an emerald. The money didn't appear to go to the parents nearby, but to a sleezy looking dwarf with an oversized bodyguard. "That's the only way he can clear *his* debt with me."

"Our king owes you a debt, young Raven King?" Aumak asked, interest piqued, her razor-sharp gaze taking his measure. "That's one for the books."

"What happens when one doesn't have an uncontracted child to pay for debts?"

"They work for the crown down in the royal mines until their debt is cleared."

"Do children ever have to go into the mines?"

"No, never," Aumak said. "King Flein demands all his subjects learn a trade."

"That's small comfort," Christoffer said, not merely referring to the dwarf king's stature.

"Very small," said Geirr.

Aumak guided them away from the square and the auctioneer. The mood was subdued as they wended their way through the cobbled streets. The colorful signs and banners beckoning passersby to their wares faded into background noise. Christoffer's thoughts were back in the square with that child, wondering: if his friends hadn't saved him, would he have been sold to a dwarf to learn a trade; or sold to work in the mines? He couldn't contemplate the horror of it. How much more distressed his mother would've been had he never returned home?

Why, just when he thought he was in an okay headspace, did the fear from that uncertain time creep back in threatening to overwhelm him? So many what-ifs and could've-beens jostled in his head. He had to remind himself that it didn't *almost* happen, because it never happened. Just like earlier with Geirr; when he hadn't been *almost* killed. He wasn't lucky then and Christoffer wasn't lucky now. It wasn't luck that saved either of them.

Zaria had found the Hart of Gloomwood Forest, and while he hadn't been what she thought she was seeking, it had saved him. Then they saved Hart. He looked to the stoic figure of Henrik in front of him. He wondered what the Stag Lord was thinking about now that he was back in the midst of Malmdor. He hadn't almost died back then, either. Near misses were still misses and Christoffer would need to remember that and not invite the other more horrible outcomes to his thoughts. Dwelling in dark places of thought would only invite more trouble.

But he still wondered a bit, despite himself. Surely as an elk, Hart hadn't been threatened with slavish servitude, but he'd not been on a picnic either. He had been wrapped in debilitating dwarfish chains and helf hostage. He was grateful and sorry for the Stag Lord's sacrifice and more grateful that he did not burden Zaria with the events from his time here. She was too tenderhearted to give such a burden to hold.

The passage grew steadily warmer and warmer as they left the commercial hub of Malmdor. The industrial district, home to a plethora of fiery furnaces, sweltered. The air was thick and shimmered with heat, at turns muggy and at others arid. Steam wafted from some forges, while waves of dry heat drifted from others like mirages, both battling for space in the too-small cavern.

At the far end of the district, large, brilliantly, blue banners hung in front of towering black metal doors. The designs on the banners left no doubt who they would find on the other side. Insignias bearing a golden hammer imposed over cerulean flame heralded the forge of the Master Gyllenhammar, home to the Gyllenhammar Flame guild.

Two sentinels guarded the outside, preventing dwarves from wandering in to spectate. They looked bored, as if those who dared to trespass on the Master Gyllenhammar's domain were few and far between. Hank sauntered down the street as if he were home. His tail wagged happily as he peered into the workshops along the way. Once in a while, a weather-wyvern would stick its nose out to stare at Hank before returning inside their forge.

Curious eyes watched their progress toward the gleaming black doors. Whenever Christoffer caught someone's gaze, most stared back, taking his measure. The constant clanging of hammers on metals echoed like an orchestra tuning their instruments, a disjointed cacophony each trying to fine-tune their craft regardless of nearby surrounding smiths. The dissonance never quite got a tone or rhythm that he could hear, but peppered with shouts and grunts, it was the sound of a bustling industry.

One of the sentinels eyed them with suspicion as they climbed the stairs to where they stood. He caught sight of Aumak and his body language changed. He crossed his hands over the spear he held, resting his chin against them. "Why hello there. It's been some time since I've seen you here, Aumak."

"Don't test me, Ragnar," she growled, waving behind her at Christoffer and his friends. "As you can see, I have business with grandmother."

"You know how incredibly busy she is running her forge and the guild. The mantle of Master Gyllenhammar isn't a light one to bear."

She prodded him in the chest with her fake hand and he winced, rubbing the tender spot. "Step aside, Ragnar, or so help me, I'll tell your girlfriend about that night down at the pub with the barmaid."

He straightened up, the playful expression on his face wiped clean. "You heartless hulder, whatever did I do to you?"

"Get in my way," she said, pushing past him. "Don't do it again if you know what's good for you."

Hank stabbed the dwarf guard in the foot with his own clawed foot, eliciting a sharp cry of pain. Ragnar hopped up and down on one foot, cussing at their retreating forms. The weather-wyvern's smug expression told all. Christoffer and Defender followed, catching up with Aumak at the heavy black metal doors.

She indicated the large ring door knocker. "Go on then, open it up."

Christoffer reached forward, grasped the handle, and tugged. The metal door resisted briefly before opening on a well-oiled sigh. Heat so hot blasted him that he discretely checked his eyebrows to ensure they hadn't been singed off.

"Oh wow," Filip said, joining him in the doorway.

Behind the door two dozen dwarves, nearly twice as many weather-wyverns, and a pair of brownies scurried back and forth in a vast warehouse-sized workshop filled with forging stations. Hammers pounded, metal scraped against metal, flames blazed brightly, machinery buzzed, and over it all, a woman's voice shouted orders.

She stood high above the activity on the floor on a metal walkway. Wispy white hair crowned her skull, tailored blue robes wrapped her small figure, an oversized golden hammer hung from her neck. Her wrinkled hands clung to the railing as she surveyed the scene. When she spotted them at the door, she crossed her arms and tapped her foot. She barked again over the noise but was too far away to be heard.

At the sound of her voice, several smiths who were closer, broke away from their tasks and headed toward her. After a brief spell of private communication, the smiths left and the Master Gyllenhammar shook back her robes. Gently clasping her hands, she proceeded with care down a series of metal steps toward the center of the room.

The three smiths approached out of nowhere, startling the group. Their burly arms and bulging muscles were more intimidating than the armored and weaponed guard outside. They looked like bouncers ready to toss them out of the coolest rager in town.

"Just remember, Princess," Aumak said warily when they stopped mere feet away. "This is what you wanted."

"It is," Zaria affirmed.

"Your doom, I suppose," she said, tensing as a much smaller figure approached. Under her breath she added, "Or maybe mine."

"Is that you, granddaughter?" the Master Gyllenhammar asked archly, parting the smiths. "You haven't come to visit me in ages. What brings this unexpected displeasure?"

Chapter Fourteen: The Gyllenhammar Flame

"Good to see you, too, grandmother," Aumak said, keeping a steadying hand on Hank's head.

"Don't call me that here," she replied, her words laced with steel. "Show respect."

"Then show me the same," Aumak said mildly, daringly. "Call me by my title."

Her grandmother sneered, "It's no longer yours. Not since you lost your hand."

"I am your heir," Aumak reminded.

"Not for long. Your brother's wife is pregnant. It could be a girl. Then I won't need you at all."

"That is your right, but until then I am still the Ember," Aumak stated calmly.

"I do not recognize you as such."

"Too bad, Soile."

Nostrils flaring in rage, the Master Gyllenhammar fought to school her expression. "You are not a member of this guild. What business do you have here? State it and be gone."

"My friends here require something only the Gyllenhammar Flame Guild can forge."

For the first time the older woman turned her gaze onto them. Her misty sight held fire and iron behind it. Christoffer knew at once their request for dragon-defying weaponry would be turned down. The Master Gyllenhammar wouldn't help them any more than she'd help her granddaughter. It was a matter of principle. She'd been feuding too long to see a different alternative. He would have to change the narrative somehow.

She sneered, "What could these youngsters want from my guild?"

Aleks and Henrik looked to Zaria to answer the old dwarf. Filip nudged her gently and she clutched her bag to her chest. After a deep fortifying breath, she said, "I am Princess Zaria of the Under Realm. My mother, Queen Helena, wishes me to take my place beside her. She sent me to get a weapon from the dwarves as great a dragon tamer as the Drakeland Sword, and –"

"No," Aumak's grandmother declared flatly. "We do not have those skills. The Drakeland Sword is unique, we could not replicate it."

Zaria's knuckles went white as she clenched her hands tighter. "I am not looking for a replica of the Drakeland Sword. One is enough, but I, as a daughter of the Under Realm, and a true sorceress, need –"

"No," she repeated. "The ability to enchant the metal to defy dragons was a skill possessed only by my husband's grandfather. It can't be done."

"But Master Gyllenhammar," Zaria protested. "We've come so far to get here. Won't you at least try? I have funds to pay you if that is what you fear."

The old dwarf clucked her tongue. "What part of no do you not understand, child?"

"The part that isn't yes," Christoffer retorted. "How can you be the greatest guild in Malmdor and Jerndor combined if you can't even consider taking on a commission like this one? Where is your sense of pride, of honor?"

Soile skewered him with a frosty look. "We do not deal in unmerited hubris. Our skills are bar none in either court of the dwarves be it high or low. We do not need to oversell our skills and open ourselves to abject humiliation. Too many guilds would take keen satisfaction in seeing us fail at such an outrageous undertaking."

"Grandmother," Aumak taunted, softly, leaning back against a pillar. "What if we take our commission elsewhere, and another guild succeeds where the Gyllenhammar Flame failed to try? The humbling you'd receive then would be colossal."

"Nobody would dare try," she said coolly. "They know their skills are no match for ours."

"I know a smith or two who'd be keen to avenge themselves and the results of their certifications. I'm sure you can think of a few, as well. Do you really want to take the chance that these children can succeed in obtaining a quality sword like the Drakeland Sword without you?"

Her granddaughter's words stilled the automatic rejection on the dwarf woman's tongue. Clenching her teeth, Soile snapped, "I will announce your commission to the guild."

Aumak's smile was more grimace. "Just don't let Regin participate, will you? The smarmy blowhard is as useful as a tang-less sword with the IQ of a goldfish."

"He passed his certification."

"At the expense of mine," Aumak retorted. "This is not his commission."

"He has as much right to apply for it as any other," Soile said dismissively and turned around. Her guards followed and Christoffer and the others took their cue from Aumak, standing still and not following.

"What now?" asked Zaria warily, when the others were out of earshot.

"My grandmother will go to the guild's vault and retrieve the necessary allotment of ore. It's precious here in Malmdor because the mines with the richest veins are all in Jerndor. The king keeps it tightly regulated and we're entirely reliant on it."

"I've been meaning to ask, does the ore go by a special name? It seems silly to call it ore all the time. What is it?" Christoffer asked.

"It's a stupid name," Aumak said, rolling her eyes. "True smiths refuse to call it by its name because it's so absurd and such an amazing display of vanity."

"Let me guess – Dwarvorian?" he offered.

Aumak snorted. "That is better than what it's really called. At least your name is for the vanity of us all."

"Oh, now I'm twice as curious, what is it?" he pressed.

She laughed. "Fleinorium."

"No way," Geirr said, laughing. "He really called it Fleinorium?"

"I'm afraid so, and before him we were forced to call it Bofurrite after his father."

"Fleinorium. Fleinorium. Fleinorium." Christoffer chanted. "It's fun to say."

Aumak grimaced. "Maybe for you."

"Bofurrite. Bofurrite. Bofurrite. Not as fun. Doesn't flow right. Not as catchy."

"The ore is renamed after each king?" Aleks asked, ending Christoffer's chanting. "Doesn't that get confusing?"

"Sometimes, but we can date pieces now by the styles and methods of forging and carbon dating the ore. The Drakeland Sword for instance was made by Bladesmith Gløder from Vidarinide."

"It's no wonder the name of the ore doesn't get used by the rest of us," Aleks said, shaking his head. "Hat's off to you for keeping it all straight."

"It's not that hard," she said, "But like I said, a smith worth his salt wouldn't use the name. It's demeaning."

Aumak's grandmother took stage again on the platform above. Using the large golden hammer on her neckless, she banged it on the metal rail. It resounded like a gong causing everyone to pause in their tracks and look up at her. She raised her hands above her head. When the whole workshop was focused on her, she spoke.

"Pride of the Gyllenhammar Flame, you have received a commission. Sorceress princess Zaria of the Under Realm wishes to procure her very own dragon taming sword akin to the Drakeland Sword. If you agree to the assignment, come collect your –" here she paused to grimace. "Fleinorium."

A murmuring took over the group as discussions winged back and forth. Of the two dozen dwarves in the forge, four broke away setting aside their current projects and stepping up to the Master Gyllenhammar. She presented to each one a massive lump of round stock, the size of a baby's forearm. The ore in this shape was not glowing with magic, so the purple sheen to it was darker, muted.

Aumak cursed softly. "Of course, Regin is among them. Notice too, how my grandmother didn't keep an allotment of ore for herself. She's refusing to participate. She was going to be your best bet, the old hag. She hasn't been given such a juicy commission in her whole career. This is out of spite."

"Or fear," Zaria said thoughtfully. "She's afraid of trying and failing, and what that failure could mean to her. She's held her position too long and doesn't want to risk it for something she already believes is impossible to do."

"Probably best she didn't take on the commission then," said Christoffer. "We wouldn't want that sentiment forged into the blade."

Aumak stared at him with a strange expression. "What an interesting thing to say," she said.

He shrugged. "It's all about intention, isn't it? The Fleinorium needs to be welded into a sword capable of defying dragons, you can't give a sword what's not in you to give."

"To your stations," Soile said, in her most imperious Master Gyllenhammar voice, thereby dismissing everyone.

The thrum of the forge as it returned to life was pleasing on the ears. A brownie in a leather smock appeared before them and bowed low. "I come to show everyone to the Master Flames."

"Thank you, Madam Brown," Aumak said. "Lead the way. If Regin is up to his usual antics let's visit him last, what do you say?"

Madam Brown tittered. "You're being unkind Miss Ember. He can't help it."

"If that smug jerk tries one more time to explain to me methods of forging that I've mastered long before he was a twinkle in his father's eye, so help me, I swear I'll toss him into his quench tank."

"See him first and you can use the other smiths as an excuse to get away," Filip said.

Aumak grinned. "Now that, I can gladly do. Present Regin to us Madam Brown."

She led them to Regin's station. He had an aide heating up the round stock while he was standing before his table and a large sheet of newsprint. The headlines on it jumped out – *200 dead elk discovered by hikers – Nature's Tragedy or Cult's Villainy? – Are these deaths omens heralding the end of times?* Christoffer itched to swipe one of the pages to read, but couldn't when Regin slapped a hand down on it, drawing everyone's attention.

"Princess," he said, his voice pleasant and not arrogant like they'd been led to believe. "It is an honor to meet you and to take on this commission. What do you picture as your sword?"

The dwarf's well-groomed beard was crisp, braided, and dark. On his head was a modern pageboy cap and his white sleeves were rolled to his muscular forearms. He licked the tip of his marker and angled down to the page, waiting for Zaria's parameters.

"Uh," she said eloquently, caught off-guard. "I'm not really sure, other than I need to be able to wield it and it must possess the same magical properties as my mother's sword."

"A fuller then," Regin said, causing Aumak to scoff. He cut her a dry glance. "You know I'm right. The princess is not her father, who the original sword was meant for, and thus, this new sword must be lighter."

"You don't need to make a broadsword either," Aumak said, crossing her arms. "What about a saber?"

"It needs to stand up to a dragon," he refuted. "Let the master work."

Her nostrils flared and her fist clenched. "Saboteur."

Ignoring her, he began sketching. After a few minutes, he spun the drawing around. "How does this design appeal to you, Princess?"

"It looks good," she said.

"It needs details," Christoffer countered. "Your mom's sword is engraved, has a guard, and a skull crusher for its pommel."

"A skull crusher?" Zaria asked with surprise. "How do you know all this, Christoffer?"

He shrugged, thinking of Flayzor, the talking sword his Dungeons and Dragons' character wielded. "I suppose you can say I like historical weapons."

"Leave those details to me," Regin said, patting the Princess' hand. "You won't be disappointed."

"Thank you, Master Flame Regin," Zaria said, slipping her hand out from under his and shaking his hand over the table. "I look forward to testing your sword."

"Shall we go to the next bladesmith?" Madam Brown asked.

"This is Master Vidis' station," Aumak said, as they wandered over.

The female dwarf on the other side of them held a hammer the size of a small club. With her shaved head, large cornflower blue eyes, and fierce expression she looked ready to do business come hell or high water. Sporting a black leather apron studded in metallic spikes and heavy boots, she rounded the table and held out her hand.

"Greetings, Princess," she stated, beckoning Zaria to sit. "My assistants will get you and your friends some refreshments."

At her words, two younger dwarves scurried off to do just that before Zaria or the others could decline. Vidis handed Zaria the round stock of Fleinorium to hold, while she readied her drawing pad. In Zaria's hands it began to glow and she quickly put it down lest she do something to damage its inherent qualities.

"Oops, sorry," she said. "I didn't mean to do that."

"That's okay Princess," Vidis said, chomping on the end of her pencil before spitting the tip of it away. "It's good to see your latent abilities engage with the ore. It means, this won't be a waste for either of us."

"That's uh, good," Zaria said a little nonplussed. "Shall I give you the parameters of the sword?"

"Hmm, no," Vidis said, shaking her head. "I want you to talk to me about your experience with Koll. I heard rumors that it was you who slayed him and with your mother's sword no less."

Confused, Zaria turned to the others. Aumak shrugged, but her keen gaze showed that her interest was piqued as well. Henrik and Aleks nodded so she turned back and gave Vidis the accounting of what happened in the Under Realm all those years ago.

When she was done, Christoffer groaned. "You forget the most important, juiciest bits! Like how Koll became your doppelganger, or that he'd spent ages perfecting his ruse! Even Filip had no idea who was who —"

"That's an outrageous and bald-faced lie," Filip swore hotly. "I asked Koll a question about our weapons and he didn't know the answer."

"I didn't have to ask," Christoffer taunted. "Koll couldn't imitate Zaria's innate goodness."

"I think I have an idea," Vidis said, interrupting them. She displayed her drawing. On the page were twin, matching blades with nesting handles and T guards.

Zaria frowned. "I'll need to wield magic too."

Geirr coughed into his hand. "Vidis is offering to make you two blades. Isn't that better than one?"

Vidis arched an eyebrow when Zaria nodded meekly. "Yes, I think you're right Geirr. Thank you, Vidis. I look forward to testing your weapons."

Madam Brown took them to the third bladesmith. This dwarf's station was littered with piles of spears. They spilled across every surface, all in various stages of completion. Her assistants moved out of the way at their approach. Aumak smiled broadly at her as they came to a stop, causing her to blush red.

"I'm Ranja. Thank you, Princess for this commission; it's been some time since we've had anything so interesting to do around here."

"Still making spears for the Ravagers?" Aumak teased, toeing one of the fallen shafts. It clacked against another before stilling.

"Always," she said. "You have to love them, but they go through my spears like sands in an hourglass. Gone before they even have a chance to appreciate their beauty and mastery."

"You could tell them not to throw them so often," Aleks said. "Those ladies should charge-in for more close combat instead of always using their spears for range attacks."

"I take it you've had dealings with them?" Ranja asked. "And you still have your limbs? Were they your allies?"

Zaria scoffed. "I can say with some confidence that no they were not."

"But they weren't enemies either. They'd been befuddled and taken advantage of by Fritjof," Henrik said. "Though it didn't make it any easier to deal with at the time, knowing who was behind their actions, helped us stay focused."

Aleks grinned and pointed to a sack on Ranja's table. "Do you feed your finished spears into that?"

She looked surprised. "You know about their bag of holding?"

"I have it," Aleks said. "At least one of them, as a prize won in battle."

Aumak covered her face and started laughing. "I knew it! Those old biddies. To think they tried to tell you that you weren't delivering on schedule."

Ranja grimaced. "Does nobody in that battalion do inventory? What a mess."

Aleks grinned. "I haven't checked it in a while, but it appears I'm now the owner of an army's worth of spears. Thank you for that."

"Take this other one," Ranja insisted, slapping the twin to his bag against his chest. "I plan to not make another spear for the rest of the year and you won't be getting any more freebies from me."

"I'll make good use of it and the spears," he promised.

"I'm sure you will. Now, Princess, while you were conversing with the other Master Flames I have made some preparatory drawings. Please look them over and tell me which ones meet your specifications."

"Thank you," Zaria said, bowing slightly as the drawings were handed over.

"That one," Christoffer said, pointing to a wavy sword with curves in it. "It looks like a dragon's body. Could you make a pommel in the shape of a dragon's head?"

"Certainly," Ranja said, taking back the drawings. "Consider it done."

"Thank you Ranja," Zaria said; she looked to him. "You too, Christoffer. I'm glad to have your help in the choosing. You seem to know what you're looking for in a sword."

He laughed ruefully. "I smelt a trap here, but I promise to let you pick the final sword for yourself."

"How good of you," she teased.

"The last Master Flame is Tage. He's a bit of a free spirit, and the only one who is not a bladesmith," Aumak said.

Madam Brown nodded. "That is true, he's more of a fabricator."

"With a flair for armor," added Aumak.

His workspace was next to Ranja's so they didn't have to cross the forge. Unlike the others he had no assistants. His table was covered in half-finished projects. Breastplates, helmets, and gauntlets lay dismantled in pieces like unfinished puzzles waiting for the missing piece to be added. He was the oldest of the dwarves taking on the challenge to forge a sword as renowned as the Drakeland Sword.

"I can make you a weapon," he told Zaria. "My price is the ability to name it if I win."

She looked at him in confusion. "Why would you want that? How can you earn a living off a name?"

"Swords of legend get names, and the legend is the living. I want nothing to do with such a pansy name as the Drakeland Sword. Don't get me wrong, Princess, but I don't trust you to name it."

"With kings renaming the same ore again and again after themselves, you're worried about the name I would choose for a sword?" she asked, incredulous and a bit offended.

He spat on the floor. "Just promise me I get to name it and I'll make you the finest damn sword that's ever been forged in these walls."

"Think twice," Henrik warned under his breath.

"Names have power," reminded Madam Brown.

"You can be part of the choosing of the name," Zaria offered. "We'll decide on it together."

"Fine," he said, grumpily. "I can see I won't persuade you to do anything less." He spat in his hand and held it out. "Go on, do the same to yours."

She did so gingerly and held out her hand. He grabbed it and pumped it once. When he let go she immediately wiped it against her pants and backed away.

"Good," Tage said, and turned back to his round stock, grabbing a piece of chalk and marking the metal. "Get out of here, I've work to do."

"What happens next?" Zaria asked Aumak.

"Now? Now they forge."

Epilogue: Dwarvish
Metallurgy Unlocked

The competition began in earnest as the four smiths broke down their round stock, cutting it up into smaller pieces and heating those bits in their forges. They sprinkled flux like confectioner's sugar over the billets before hammers pounded, moving the heated metal into useable billets.

Curious smiths, who hadn't joined the competition wandered over to the competing dwarves' stations. Without prompting, most offered criticisms and encouragement.

"The meddling nincompoops," Aumak said in disgust. "All of them should be vying for the honor. It's been over a thousand years since a commission of this caliber has come their way."

"Is failure such a terrible thing?" Aleks asked aloud.

"It's a matter of '*honor*,'" she said with air quotes. "Even here where they're considered the *crème de la crème* of smiths, they can't stand the idea of losing face. This place used to be about learning and growing and enjoying the comradery of fellow, brilliantly talented smiths. Of making each other better.

"Sure, they're offering advice, but look a little deeper. They're really tearing down those smiths who took the commission. If anything goes wrong and if there are flaws within the blade, each and every non-competing smith is going to whisper 'I told you so. You should've listened when I said to do this or that.'"

"They're hovering like butterflies, flitting back and forth between the four forges," Henrik said. "Should we run interference? Are they hurting our chances of a good blade?"

Aumak shook her head and crossed her arms. "Let them beat their wings into nothing. They'll burn up in jealousy once one of these smithies succeeds."

One of the hovering Master Flames at Ranja's station whispered something. She flinched and dropped her billet on the ground. The dwarves around her laughed cruelly as she scrambled on the floor to pick it up. Aumak started, as if preparing to join the fray to help her before forcing herself to stand down.

"Never bring a sword to a butterfly fight," Christoffer said with sympathy.

"She'll just have to prove them all wrong, that's all," Aumak said.

"Someone will," he said, eyeing her vibrating form. "I'm sure of it." Under his breath he added, "It just may not be who you think it is."

Thanks for Reading

My dearest fiercelings, thank you for following me faithfully on this journey as we race toward the ever-nearing finish line for Christoffer's story and that also of the main series. I am truly grateful beyond measure. Please consider sharing your love of Christoffer and the gang by leaving a review at your favorite online retailer or reader website.

An Invitation

Stay in touch! You can subscribe to my free author newsletter at my website. If you do, you'll learn about upcoming releases, get behind-the-scenes information, and more.

The Adventure Continues:

Christoffer Johansen
and the Witch's Envelope

Get a sneak peek of the next book in the Zaria Fierce world, featuring Christoffer's adventures:

https://keiragillett.com/book/witchs-envelope/

About the Author and Artist:
Keira Gillett

When Keira Gillett isn't writing, she's snuggled in a blanket reading her favorite web comics or watching her favorite shows. On one side is a batch of deliciously air-popped, buttered popcorn and on the other side, eagerly waiting for a kernel or two to drop, is her shiba inu, Oskar, who knows she learned to make popcorn from Grandpaw (and that its delicious.) You can follow Keira and Oskar on Instagram with the #oskarpie hashtag.

Find Keira at https://keiragillett.com/

About the Cartographer:
Kaitlin Statz

Kaitlin Statz grew up in many different places, but currently lives in Sarasota, FL with her partner, Travis, and their young dog, Eezo. She attended New College of Florida and the University of Oxford for a life in the sciences before returning to her true love, art. She started her work as Statz Ink in 2015 and has been creating art ever since.

Find her at http://www.statzink.com/